answers in the pages

ALSO BY DAVID LEVITHAN

Boy Meets Boy

The Realm of Possibility

Are We There Yet?

The Full Spectrum (edited with Billy Merrell)

Marly's Ghost (illustrated by Brian Selznick)

Nick & Norah's Infinite Playlist (written with Rachel Cohn)

Wide Awake

Naomi and Ely's No Kiss List (written with Rachel Cohn)

How They Met, and Other Stories

The Likely Story series (written as David Van Etten, with David Ozanich and Chris Van Etten)

Love Is the Higher Law

Will Grayson, Will Grayson (written with John Green)

Dash & Lily's Book of Dares (written with Rachel Cohn)

The Lover's Dictionary

Every You, Every Me (with photographs by Jonathan Farmer)

Every Day

Invisibility (written with Andrea Cremer)

Two Boys Kissing

Another Day

Hold Me Closer: The Tiny Cooper Story

You Know Me Well (written with Nina LaCour)

The Twelve Days of Dash & Lily (written with Rachel Cohn)

Sam & Ilsa's Last Hurrah (written with Rachel Cohn)

Someday

Mind the Gap, Dash & Lily (written with Rachel Cohn)

The Mysterious Disappearance of Aidan S. (as told to his brother)

Take Me with You When You Go (written with Jennifer Niven)

DAVID LEVITHAN

answers

in the

pages

Alfred A. Knopf
New York

THIS IS A BORZOI BOOK PUBLISHED BY ALFRED A. KNOPF

Visit us on the Web! rhcbooks.com

Educators and librarians, for a variety of teaching tools, visit us at RHTeachersLibrarians.com

Library of Congress Cataloging-in-Publication Data is available upon request.
ISBN 978-0-593-48468-5 (trade) — ISBN 978-0-593-48469-2 (lib. bdg.) —
ISBN 978-0-593-48470-8 (ebook) — ISBN 978-0-593-56834-7 (intl. pbk.)

The text of this book is set in 11.25-point Apollo MT Pro.
Interior design by Cathy Bobak

Printed in the United States of America
10 9 8 7 6 5 4 3 2 1
First Edition

For Nancy Garden.

I, like so many others, am proud to have followed your loving path, hoping to leave many paths behind us both.

1

In the end, after everything they'd been through, there was only one thing the residents of Sandpiper Township could agree upon: that all the fighting, all the commotion, all the rallying came down to how a person chose to read a single sentence.

The sentence in question was:

> *At that moment Rick knew just how deeply he loved Oliver, and Oliver knew just how deeply he loved Rick, and the understanding of this moment would lead them to much of the happiness and adventure that came next.*

As sentences go, it was a bit long, and you had to read an entire book in order to get to it. Many of the residents of Sandpiper Township wouldn't have noticed it if it had been said during a TV show or appeared as a quote in the middle of a newspaper article. But because it was the last line of *The Adventurers,* and because *The Adventurers* had been assigned in Mr. Howe's fifth-grade class, people did take notice. Only one person at first, then considerably more.

It's worth reading the sentence again before I begin to tell you what happened.

> At that moment Rick knew just how deeply he loved Oliver, and Oliver knew just how deeply he loved Rick, and the understanding of this moment would lead them to much of the happiness and adventure that came next.

It would be a good idea for you to stop and consider what you think about this sentence. This will be the last time you get to read it without other people telling you what *they* think about it.

That's how it was in Sandpiper Township that November. I know this because I was one of the first people in Sandpiper Township besides Mr. Howe to read the sentence. Unfortunately, I didn't read it as soon as I could have. I brought the book home with me and only read the first few pages. Then I left it on the kitchen counter and went to eat a snack in front of the TV.

From there, it only took an hour for my life to spiral out of control.

one

Gideon White was only really, really good at two things: playing with words and collecting turtles. Of the turtles, only one of them, Samson, was an actual living, breathing (*as much as turtles could be seen breathing) turtle. All the others were glass turtles or stone turtles or plastic turtles he'd gathered from gift shops, toy stores, and craft fairs.

As for the words Gideon played with—most of them were living and breathing too, but Gideon often felt he was the only person who noticed this.

Right now, it was Gideon's job to feed the only living, breathing turtle in his room and to dust all the others. Gideon's mother claimed to be allergic to dust, which Gideon thought was an exaggeration, since dust was everywhere and if she were truly allergic to dust she'd be coughing or sneezing or wheezing every second of every day. Instead, all she really did was complain about the dust, even when it wasn't there.

Samson was not Gideon's best friend, but he was definitely the friend Gideon trusted most. A lot of this had to do with the fact that Samson was a turtle and couldn't talk. Gideon's other two best friends, Joelle and Tucker, talked all the time. He couldn't tell Joelle anything without Tucker finding out about it, and vice versa. Which saved Gideon some time, not having to explain things twice. But it was still annoying that he had to assume anything he said would echo beyond where it was meant to go.

Joelle and Tucker were both in Ms. June's fifth-grade class. The alphabet had allowed them to sit next to each other while Gideon was banished to the back row. When Debbie Weiss had left class because her father got a job in Arizona, Gideon thought he'd at least be able to move up a row, which would have gotten him one desk closer to Tucker. But instead Ms. June kept the space empty. Gideon didn't ask her why. He didn't ask Ms. June anything, if he could avoid it.

Gideon spent most of his time in class finding new words within the ones Ms. June wrote on the board. So if she wrote *history homework,* he would scramble up its letters to find phrases like *my stork* or *Who is more Thor?* or *He took my sow!* He might even try to turn multiple words into one simpler word, like *histomework.* He'd do all of this in his head because early in the year he'd tried writing it all down and Ms. June had caught him doing it and instead of thinking he was doing something smart, she treated him like he was doing something wrong. That had put an end to writing it down.

Gideon was lost finding words in Benedict Arnold's name (*red coat, need cab, tied boar*) when he felt the room around him pause, which meant he needed to pay attention. He raised his head and saw a boy standing next to Debbie Weiss's old desk. The boy had shaggy hair and a bright green shirt, and looked at Gideon for a second before sitting down. Gideon had no idea who this boy was, and from looking around he realized that Ms. June had just introduced him to the class, and Gideon had missed it entirely.

For the next half hour, Gideon stared at the back of the boy's head and tried to figure out his last name. Since Dana Wachtel was sitting in front of the boy, Gideon assumed the last name had to be alphabetically located somewhere between Wachtel and White.

Warner.

Watson.

Webster.

Weeble.

Westing.

Wheelmaker.

Whippoorwill.

Gideon tried to sneak a look inside the boy's book bag, to see if there was a name on anything in there. But it was zipped closed.

The boy was sitting up straight. Paying attention to Ms. June.

Or maybe just appearing to pay attention. Because Gideon could see the top right corner of the boy's notebook.

He watched as the boy drew a cat. Then a bull. Then a rabbit. Then . . . a turtle.

Gideon wanted to warn the boy to hide the notebook from Ms. June if he didn't want to get in trouble. But he also really liked the turtle and didn't want the boy to turn the page.

When it was time for lunch, the boy shuffled his notebook into his bag and jumped out of the room as soon as he could. Gideon started packing up his own books and saw something on the board he hadn't noticed before.

A new name.

Not someone from the Revolutionary War, like Benedict Arnold.

No. It had to be the boy's name.

Roberto Garcia.

CHAPTER ONE:
UP IN SMOKE!

Rick Mason knew he had about five minutes left to live . . .
if he was lucky.

There was something about being handcuffed to a chair
in the heart of an abandoned building about to be set on fire
that forced him to focus. It didn't matter that Rick was only
twelve years old—his mind often felt much older than that,
and at this moment it only had one purpose: to get him out
of that house.

It had been a mistake to come to the mansion alone, and
an even greater mistake to let his guard down for even a
second. Of course McAllister had sent his bodyguards to
do the dirty work. By the time Rick had heard the telltale
lunge of boots, the crowbar was already swinging toward
his head. They could have done away with him then . . .
but clearly McAllister wanted Rick to experience a more
elaborate death than a simple pummeling. Rick was starting

to smell the smoke now. This wasn't the time to dwell on mistakes.

First step: Break the chair.

Rick tipped forward on his feet, then flipped himself into the air. When he landed, he made sure to lean all his weight onto the chair's wooden frame. The first fall weakened it. The second fall cracked it. The third fall broke it. Rick's spine also felt like it might scatter onto the floor, but Rick clenched his teeth and kept going. The sound of fire from the ground floor was beginning to roar now, and the smoke was getting heavy. Rick swiped his cuffed hands on the floor and was relieved when they came up without any gasoline on them. McAllister wanted this to look like a natural death. It bought Rick a little time.

The cuffs would have to stay on for now. He pulled his shirt over his nose and mouth, then dropped low, pushing forward to the staircase.

Unfortunately, the fire had gotten there first, and was now climbing its way to him.

This left the windows. At the top of the stairway was a stained-glass casement with a saint in the middle. Saint Christopher, Rick thought, even though Saint Christopher really wasn't McAllister's type. Like many Adventurers, Rick had a great respect for art. In this case, it meant he whispered a quick apology to the glassmakers before crashing through their creation.

Rick was relieved to find the mansion's front overhang waiting underneath the shattered window.

He was not relieved when he noticed that people were shooting at him.

And the front porch was on fire.

The smoke gave him some cover, but it also meant that the place where he was standing was likely to cave in, in about five . . . four . . . three . . . two . . .

Rick ran around a corner and leapt in the direction of the tree line. Had it been winter, he would've landed on ice-hard ground. But it was still enough of autumn for there to be leaves to soften his plunge. With shots inconsiderately pinging off the tree trunks to his left and his right, he zipped deep into the forest, only catching his breath when he heard the sound of a fire brigade making its way onto the property.

Awkwardly (because of the handcuffs) he checked his pocket watch. It was twenty strokes short of six. He had to keep moving. Not just because McAllister's goons would be on his tail in the time it took to lick a lollipop, but because he prided himself on never missing a rendezvous. McAllister might manage to kill Rick Mason, but he would *not* make him late.

Nineteen minutes later, Rick approached the back of a Texaco station, relieved that none of the attendants had chosen this moment for a coffee break. Two minutes later, a motorcycle swerved to his side.

Rick knew better than to say a word until Oliver removed his helmet.

Once it was off and Rick could see Oliver's smile as well as his smiling eyes, he chided, "You're late."

Oliver took this in stride. "You didn't tell me you were leaving. Didn't even leave a note on your bed." He registered Rick's situation. "And you definitely didn't tell me to fetch the bolt cutter."

"Mistakes were made," Rick mumbled as Oliver handed him a helmet.

"But I knew to come here anyway," Oliver said, neither annoyed nor surprised. They both put on their helmets.

Rick hopped onto the seat behind Oliver. Then, because there was no other way to do it, he brought his cuffed arms around Oliver's head and got them around his waist.

"Hold on," Oliver said, gunning the motor.

Rick knew there'd be enough time to figure out what had gone wrong. Right now, he was grateful that this one thing had gone right. Rick Mason was an orphan, but that didn't mean he lived a life bereft of family. Part of being an Adventurer was knowing the other Adventurers had your back. Or, in this case, would give you his own back to hang on to as you zoomed your way to safety.

2

My mom came and stood in front of the TV.

"What is this?" she said, holding out the book I'd left on the counter.

"A book for school. I'll start reading it later."

I figured I was in trouble for choosing TV over a book. So I was definitely surprised when my mom said, "I'm not so sure about that, Donovan."

I honestly thought I'd misheard her. This couldn't possibly be *my* mother, telling me *not* to read.

She went on, though, asking me, "How far have you gotten?"

"We read the beginning in class."

"Which class?"

"Um . . . English. I mean, language arts. Which is the same thing as English."

I thought, okay, she must have started reading it, and

probably felt it was too violent for fifth graders. Or maybe it was too fun. I could see her objecting to that. Sometimes Mr. Howe made us read these old classics that had cobwebs between each of the sentences, but other times he'd have us read a more recent book, even one that didn't have any shiny award seals on the cover. With this book, he'd said we were starting an adventure unit, and what better place to start an adventure unit than with a book called *The Adventurers*?

"I would like to read some more of it, and would like to understand some things about the author before you continue," my mother told me now.

She almost made it sound like she was asking my permission.

She was definitely not asking my permission.

I figured, *I guess I'll just go back to watching TV.* But instead she turned off the TV and told me to do the rest of my homework. She actually said, "Go do your math homework." Because maybe she figured that was the opposite of language arts.

I went to my room . . . but I kept the door open so I could hear her getting on the phone, calling some of my friends' moms, the ones she was friends with. Like Sean's mom. And Tarah's mom. But not Allison's mom. I couldn't hear what she was saying, exactly, but I could hear the names Rick and Oliver coming up a lot. From the chapter Mr. Howe had read to us, I remembered those were the names of the characters from the book. I expected to hear my mom talking about the bullets flying and the fact that two twelve-year-olds were clearly driving a motorcycle without a license. (At least they wore helmets. I definitely would have understood her screaming if they hadn't worn helmets.)

But that wasn't what she was angry about.

The thing is, my mom doesn't read books like I read books. I like to be surprised, so I try to avoid even the summary on the back. My mom, though, doesn't like to be surprised. So she'll read a few pages at the start, to get a sense of what the book is about, and then she'll read the last page, so she knows where it's going. If she's happy with that, she'll return to the beginning and keep reading.

It wasn't until right before dinner, when my dad got home and she asked him if they could talk for a second in private, that I remembered the last-page-first thing. That's when I knew: It wasn't the start of the book that had made her take the book away from me. It must have been something about the ending. But I didn't have the book anymore, so I wasn't able to read the ending myself to see if I was right.

It wasn't until the next day, when I was back in Mr. Howe's class, that I'd read the sentence the whole town would soon be arguing about.

two

Gideon didn't tell his turtle Samson about the new kid, because for the first few days, he didn't find out much about him.

It wasn't that Roberto was quiet, exactly. He answered whenever Ms. June called on him. At lunch, he fit right into the boy table, and since the boys around him didn't ask many questions, there weren't many answers provided. Gideon had heard him say the word *Florida,* so that could have been where he was from. Or maybe that was just where his grandparents lived. Or he was talking with the boys at the boy table about a Florida sports team. (*Gideon assumed there were sports teams in Florida even if he couldn't name one himself.)

Gideon, Tucker, and Joelle always sat at the boy-girl table so they could be together. If Gideon's curiosity about Roberto was brimming, Joelle's was about halfway to the top and Tucker's hadn't been poured at all.

"What do you think about the new kid?" Gideon asked them at the end of Roberto's first week.

"He seems nice," Joelle said.

"I haven't really noticed," Tucker mumbled before turning his attention back to his potato chips.

"He likes to wear green," Gideon observed. (*It was true. Four out of five days, Roberto had either worn a green shirt or a shirt with green stripes.)

"That's weird," Tucker said.

"Why?" Joelle asked. "Maybe he likes green."

"No," Tucker said. "I mean it's weird that Gideon noticed. Do you keep track of everyone's clothes?"

The answer was no, but only because Tucker had said *everyone's*. Meaning, the whole class. Gideon did not keep track of the whole class's clothes. He kept track of Ms. June's because he was forced to look at her so often and he had to make the most of the time spent eyes-forward. And sometimes he still kept track of what Tucker wore. He used to do it much more often, back when their best-friend group was a duo instead of a trio. He'd even try to guess what Tucker would be wearing before he got to school.

He never told Tucker about this. But maybe this curiosity about Roberto was a little bit like it had been at first with Tucker. Maybe this was start-of-friendship curiosity. With Tucker, it had lasted until Joelle. Then, once the three of them were the three of them, Gideon had felt the curiosity subside, like how when you move into a new house and get a new bedroom at first it's really intense and you spend a lot of time thinking about it, but then after a while it just becomes . . . your room.

It made a little more sense to Gideon then, to think that his curiosity was coming from friendship. Or wanting to be friends, since he and Roberto hadn't really talked to each other yet, and Gideon knew that friends needed to talk to each other to be friends (*with an exception when one of the friends is a turtle).

"He's been sitting next to Carrie on the bus home," Joelle told Gideon and Tucker, keeping her voice low. "He told her he likes movies, and when she asked him some of his favorites, he mentioned a few she didn't know. But he said *Lion King* was the best Disney movie. She said her favorite was *Beauty and the Beast* and he said he liked that one, too."

Gideon tried to absorb these facts. And then, when he was back in class and Roberto was sitting down in front of him, he tried to keep these facts to himself, because if he suddenly blurted out, "Why do you like *The Lion King* more than *Beauty and the Beast*?" he'd have to explain to Roberto how he knew that Roberto preferred *The Lion King,* and then he'd have to explain why he and Joelle had been talking about Roberto in the first place.

So Gideon kept quiet. He studied the back of Roberto's neck. *The nape,* he thought, pleased to know the word for it but also confused about why the back of the neck had its own word but the side of the neck didn't. (*The front, he figured, was the throat, which wasn't nearly as exciting a word as *nape*. Which could be rearranged into *pane,* like a window you could stare at to try to figure out what was on the other side.)

To distract himself from this distraction, Gideon tried to rearrange all the letters in Alexander Hamilton's name into phrases.

All hen exit and roam

A tiller exam on hand

Lion, relax and math

After a few minutes of this, frustrated by his meager results, he moved on to Roberto's name, to find the words inside it.

Root

Bet

Too

Boot

Ore

Robe

"Gideon?"

Roberto was staring at him. Well, not really *staring*. But he had turned around and was passing a worksheet back.

"Thank you!" Gideon hastily exclaimed. In the whole classroom, he was the only kid who said thank you when handed this particular worksheet, with an enthusiasm usually reserved for large presents.

Roberto smiled and said, "You're welcome." Then he kept

looking-not-staring as Gideon took the paper out of his hand and set it on his desk.

It wasn't a big interaction. It didn't last more than ten seconds—twenty seconds, tops.

But in this interaction, Gideon had learned two important things:

(1) Roberto had dimples when he smiled.

and

(2) Roberto knew Gideon's name.

Jumping to . . .

CHAPTER FOUR: PROTECTING THE CODE

Melody Tam was bright and resourceful enough to be an Adventurer . . . she just chose not to be one.

"Maybe I want to have adventures on my own," she told Rick and Oliver. "Adventures you'll never know about."

Rick wasn't sure how he felt about that. But he wasn't about to pick a fight with Melody. Whenever he picked a fight with Melody, Melody won. It wasn't even close.

The three of them were sitting in the RV that acted as their Adventurers headquarters, parked in an unobtrusive underground warren beneath Rick's grandparents' property. As Rick lounged on the sofa and Melody perched on a chair, Oliver hung in the background, cleaning counters and straightening books on shelves. There was something about Melody's presence that made Oliver want the trailer to be a little less messy than it ordinarily was.

"You know you're not safe here, right?" Melody was

saying. "McAllister isn't going to stop until you hand over the Doomsday Code."

Rick's expression became a storm cloud. "My parents died for that Code. McAllister is never going to get it."

Oliver tried to fade even further into the background, his pale skin getting even paler. Even though Melody was often their partner in adventure, she still hadn't picked up on the fact that Rick's memory was lousy, a cage with bars set too far apart. He would never have been able to remember a monumentally long sequence like the Doomsday Code. Most people couldn't.

So Oliver had memorized it instead, because Oliver's memory didn't have bars—it had walls.

The storm cloud passed, and Rick beamed again, sitting up proudly, his dark skin glowing with sudden excitement.

"We're headed to Yellowstone," he said. "We'll blend in well there. And we can put together our plan to take down McAllister once and for all."

It was clear to Oliver that Rick wanted to impress Melody. Her refusal to be enchanted by Rick was paradoxically enchanting *to* Rick. And Oliver had to imagine that there was some interest on Melody's part as well. Otherwise, why would she keep coming back?

A sly smile now insinuated itself onto her face. "I've always wanted to see El Capitan," she said, leaning forward.

"Well, why don't you come climb it with us?" Rick replied, leaning forward as well.

"That's Yosemite," Oliver mumbled from the kitchen area. "Yellowstone has Old Faithful. And . . . bears."

Suddenly, the air was cut by a klaxon coming from the security console. Oliver was standing closest, so he was the one who imparted the information to his friends:

"We have a truck approaching the gates."

Rick was behind him now, studying the camera's footage. "Looks like it's just UPS."

Oliver went to touch the screen for a heat scan, but Melody beat him to it.

The heat scan showed that there were at least ten armed adults in the back of the truck.

"That's one heck of a delivery," Melody quipped.

Rick grinned at her, his dimples giving every word he said natural quotation marks.

"Guess you're along for the ride," he told her.

"Seat belts!" Oliver called out, jumping into the driver's seat and activating the hologram that would make it look like a middle-aged woman was driving.

Aboveground, there was an explosion as McAllister's forces blew up the front gate.

"Must be an urgent delivery," Rick mused.

"Well," Oliver said, "I hope they don't require a signature."

Melody laughed, and when Oliver looked in the rearview mirror, he could see the friendly look she was giving him. Then he broke their glance, because there were more

21

important things to think about, like escape. Without another word, he gunned the engine and sped them through the escape tunnel. A mile later, they broke out into the sunlight. On the security monitors they could see McAllister's forces shooting at lawn decorations out of frustration. They knew nobody was home.

"To Yosemite!" Rick called out.

"Yellowstone!" Melody and Oliver corrected at the same time. It was almost as if their voices were holding hands.

"Yes, el capitan," Rick said lightly in response.

3

My mother drove me to school the next day. She was in a pretty good mood, and even let me put on music instead of listening to her morning talk guy. She commented on what nice weather it was and suggested I see if some friends wanted to go to the park after school. It was all very friendly, but I was still a little scared. Mom had a very determined look in her eye, and both my father and I knew that when Mom had a very determined look in her eye, it was better to ride the wave than try to stand against it.

There was the time when I was in second grade when she'd convinced the PTA that bake sales were really just a way to get kids hooked on processed sugar, so instead of a usual bake sale they had a "make sale" where parents sold healthy dinners to raise money for a new roof for the school gymnasium. Then, when I was in third grade and they wanted to name the gymnasium after a local businessman who'd donated a lot of money to the roof, she'd led the petition drive to name it after "a good American historical figure" instead, because she said it sent the wrong message to us kids to say that all it took was wealth to get recognition, and also the local businessman had made a lot of his money from a chain of liquor stores. Which is how we ended up playing dodgeball in the Dwight D. Eisenhower Gymnasium.

Normally Mom would drop me off at the front door, but today she parked the car and walked in with me. She didn't tell me what she planned to do, but she didn't really need to. I could guess. While I went off to my classroom, she would head to the principal's office.

The truth was, my mother had spent far more time in the principal's office than I had. Sometimes it was just for meetings—whenever there was a committee or a task force for parents, Mom would volunteer. But other times, she went to the principal's office because she felt it was her job to tell her what the school could be doing better. The cafeteria food could be more nutritious. The holiday concert could contain some holiday music instead of songs from the radio. A committee could be formed to fundraise for a new jungle gym because the one we climbed on at recess looked like it was about to topple.

I never knew about these conversations when they were happening. I only heard about them when my mom complained to my dad over dinner.

The big difference this time was that Mom had brought a

prop—my copy of *The Adventurers*, which she was holding like a stone she was about to put in a slingshot.

"Have a great day, sweetie," she said to me when we got to the point in the hall where I'd go left and she'd go straight.

I smiled at her and even gave her a little wave. But it was definitely hard to feel like I was having a great day when I walked into Mr. Howe's class.

Mr. Howe must have noticed the dread on my face. "Is there something wrong, Donovan?" he asked.

I shook my head and sat down.

My friend Kira sat in front of me, and when I saw *The Adventurers* poking out of her backpack, I asked if I could borrow it for a few minutes.

"Don't you have yours?" she asked back.

"I left it at home," I lied.

She handed it over. Her bookmark was at the start of the second chapter, where we'd left off. Even though I knew it would spoil the story, I turned to the very end.

I wasn't sure what to expect—there were many possibilities for what could have made my mother take the book away from me. Violence, definitely. But even worse, the characters could have started cursing. There were some words that Mom thought were curse words but nobody else really thought were curse words—while she wouldn't have liked finding one of those, I wasn't sure that would have set off her alarms. So that meant it had to be a BIG curse word. Or maybe . . . *a lot of them.*

I started looking on the last page, but couldn't find any. Then I turned to the start of the last chapter and scanned through.

Nothing.

It wasn't a very violent scene, either. And there weren't any signs of blasphemy that I could find. It was after the adventure was over, and Rick and Oliver seemed to be ready to go off on another adventure.

I went to the second-to-last chapter and couldn't find any curse words there. I was very confused.

Kira was also confused. I hadn't realized she was looking at me. But now she asked, "Do you always read books like that?"

"Uh, no," I said. I almost added, *My mom does,* but I was worried that mentioning my mom would actually summon her to the doorway of the classroom. So I kept my mouth shut, except to say thank you as I handed the book back.

The bell rang and everyone sat down at their desks. We didn't have language arts until the afternoon, so there wasn't any mention of *The Adventurers.* Instead we had to take out our math homework.

As Mr. Howe walked us through equations on the board, I kept looking to the door, expecting my mother or Principal Woodson or—worst of all—both of them to show up. It was only after about an hour had passed that I started to relax. Maybe my mother had thought she'd read a curse word in the book and Principal Woodson had pointed out there wasn't actually one there.

Now the big problem was that I didn't have the book with me and I was going to have to tell Mr. Howe that I'd left it at home. Which shouldn't have been a big problem—kids left books at home all the time. The problem was that I wasn't usually one of those kids. I never left my book or my homework behind. I was very proud of that. So it felt wrong to be caught out on something that wasn't my fault.

At recess I asked permission to go to the library, which meant I was leaving our basketball game one player short . . . but I figured if I was quick, maybe I'd get ten minutes on the court at the end.

With a wave to Ms. Guy when I walked in, I went straight to the fiction section and found my way to *Bright, G. R.* The only book of his that was there was *The Adventurers,* and there were two hardcover copies. I flipped to the back of one and saw that only one person had signed it out in the past year. I was about to make that two.

Ms. Guy looked at me funny when she saw what I was checking out.

"Aren't you reading this in Mr. Howe's class?" she asked.

"I don't have my copy today," I told her. I didn't say that I'd forgotten it or left it at home. I didn't want Ms. Guy to think I'd do that, either.

She scanned the book and gave it to me.

"Well, return it when you get your copy back. And no taking notes in the margins!"

I was deeply offended that she would think I'd even

consider writing in a book. But since I was in a hurry to get back to recess, I just said, "I won't!" and ran back out.

I didn't notice anything unusual at first when we returned from recess. It wasn't until we got to language arts that I saw Mr. Howe was looking at me a little more than he usually did. He asked everyone to take out their books . . . and then looked surprised when I took out a copy. I could tell he was about to ask me how I'd gotten it, but then he must have seen that it was a hardcover and had the clear library wrapping over it.

Before asking us to read aloud, he wrote the word *Adventure* on the board and asked us what we thought it meant. Different kids said "It's when you're running for your life" and "It's when you're out of your normal life and doing things you never thought you'd do" and "It's a really exciting trip you take that's also full of danger." Then Mr. Howe said we were right on target, telling us the dictionary definition was "an unusual and exciting, typically hazardous, experience or activity." I liked the phrase *typically hazardous*. It definitely seemed to apply to what was happening in the book.

Mr. Howe then asked us who we liked to go on adventures with. When people started shouting out friends' names, Mr. Howe said, "Okay, who else besides your friends?"

Hesitantly, Amelia Song said, "My parents?"

A few people giggled at that, and Curtis King yelled out, "No way!"

Then Bryan Cart said, "Grandparents!" and a lot of kids agreed with him.

I was glad Mr. Howe didn't call on me, because when I thought about the definition, I wasn't sure I really *had* gone on any adventures. But I wasn't about to admit that.

Mr. Howe started reading chapter two out loud. Rick and Oliver were riding their motorcycle to safety . . . but then a helicopter appeared on the horizon and they were in a chase again. After he'd read a few pages, Mr. Howe started calling on kids to take over reading. I always liked reading out loud in class . . . but this time I wasn't one of the kids chosen. We got to a point in the chapter when Rick and Oliver were racing toward a tunnel, because the helicopter couldn't follow them there. But there were also headlights in the tunnel coming toward them—a train! In a split second, they had to make a choice—

And that's where Mr. Howe stopped us for the day. A few kids groaned loudly and others protested. But Mr. Howe said it was time to go to gym. Then he said something that didn't strike me as odd at the time, but of course now strikes me as very odd. He told everyone to be sure to take their books home tonight, and to keep them there tomorrow, since we would be doing something different in language arts tomorrow afternoon. We should finish reading chapters two and three over the weekend, and we'd resume our discussion on Monday.

I debated whether or not to leave my library copy in my desk. The idea of bringing it home made my heart start to beat a little faster than usual. But then I thought it would be weird if everyone else had their copies and I didn't have one, so I put it deep in my book bag. When I got home, I felt I was carrying something radioactive into the house. I ran up to my room and shut the door dramatically, even though both of my parents were at work. Then I started reading, as much as I could before they got home.

When I heard the garage door, I quickly marked my place in chapter four and put the book under my bed, in a box full of cars and action figures. It was a good thing I did, too, because as soon as she was home, Mom stopped by my bedroom to see what I was doing.

I gestured to my book bag and told her I was about to start my homework.

"Do it at your desk, not on the floor," she admonished. Then, taking a softer tone, she said, "I spoke to your principal today about the book your teacher assigned, and its inappropriate content. She said she needed to read the book before passing judgment, and I told her I understood that. But she better be a quick reader, because I know I'm not the only parent she's going to be hearing from. Many of us are upset by this."

Upset by what? I wanted to ask. But really, I didn't want to have anything to do with whatever they were doing.

I'd read the book and find out for myself.

In secret.

three

Strangely enough, it was Ms. June who brought Gideon and Roberto together.

It was time for the class to read a new book for language arts. (*Most of the other kids made fun of the name *language arts*, but Gideon liked the idea that you could use words to paint or sculpt or compose.) Ms. June announced that the class would be doing a group project, so the students would need to divide into pairs. (*Gideon didn't think a *pair* counted as a *group*, but it was useless to argue with Ms. June on points like this.)

Ms. June held up a copy of *Harriet the Spy*. Some kids in the class cheered, because they'd already read it. Other kids in the class groaned, because they'd already read it.

"This was my favorite book when I was your age," Ms. June confided. "I know some of you might be familiar with it . . . but I have to tell you, there's something important about going back to books you've already read. You will always find new things inside, or have new reactions to characters you thought you already knew well. You learn more about the story and you also learn more about yourself as a reader, and where you are in life. I still find new things every time I read this book, and I'm hoping you will, too."

Gideon hadn't read the book before. He vaguely recalled that kids in Ms. Kerr's third-grade class had read it. But he'd had Mr. Bravehorse, and they'd read *Mrs. Frisby and the Rats of NIMH* instead. (*This hadn't bothered Gideon, because *Mrs. Frisby and the Rats of NIMH* was also a really good book. For the first time, he realized teachers had a hard job, deciding which really good books to teach, since there were definitely more really good books than there were days in the school year.)

Ms. June continued. "The first year I taught this book, I assigned kids to be like Harriet. I asked them to spy on the people around them, keeping notes in a notebook they'd then share with the class. This turned out to be a *huge* mistake, so I want to make clear to you now—our project will *not* be to spy on people."

A few kids groaned at this news. Gideon couldn't tell whether it was the same kids who'd groaned earlier or whether it was the kids who'd cheered before who were now groaning.

"I promise, there will still be an element of spy-like observation to the assignment," Ms. June said in response. "But to start, I need you each to pick a partner."

Pick a partner. At first, Gideon didn't totally comprehend what this meant. But then there was a sudden burst of noise in the classroom as kids started leaning over to their friends, or calling out across the room to their friends, and Gideon knew he had maybe five seconds to do what he wanted, and before he could think about it too much, he was reaching out his hand, and that hand was tapping Roberto on the shoulder and then moving back slightly as Roberto turned around, looking more relieved than confused, and again before he could think about it too much, Gideon was asking Roberto if he wanted to be partners and Roberto was saying yes, and then they were both dangling there because now that the decision had been made, they weren't sure exactly what they needed to do next. Then Ms. June asked if anyone hadn't found a partner, and Gideon was amazed because he wasn't one of the few kids raising a hand.

"Have you read it before?" Roberto asked as Ms. June did the remaining pairing.

Gideon shook his head.

"It's really good," Roberto said. "I'm excited to read it again."

Because of the title, Gideon asked, "Is it about a girl who works for the government? Like James Bond?"

Roberto laughed, but not in a way that made Gideon feel stupid. "No. It's more about the neighborhood and all the stories you find by paying attention to what's going on around you. Well, find or make up. But I don't want to give too much away if you haven't read it!"

Roberto was excited talking about the book, and that made Gideon excited, both about the book and about being friends with Roberto.

Ms. June called for everyone's attention, and the class became quiet as she passed out the books and told everyone to read the first chapter by Thursday. She didn't explain any more about what the "group project" was going to be. Usually, this would have bothered Gideon—he liked assignments to be specific. But right now he was content to know he had a good partner and that it was a good book.

The rest would follow.

Jumping to . . .

CHAPTER SEVEN:
CAGE MATCH!

"Well," Rick said, "this is certainly not a great way to spend a Tuesday."

He and Oliver were dangling in separate cages over the most powerful thermal geyser in Yellowstone—one so destructive that tourists weren't allowed anywhere near it. Only someone as rich as McAllister could get access. ("I told them it was for a private wedding," he'd cackled as the cages were brought in.) According to a placard that Rick and Oliver had been marched past, there was a scalding eruption due in exactly ten minutes.

"We should have gone to Yosemite," Oliver mumbled.

"I shouldn't have sent those postcards," Rick mumbled back. How else could they have been tracked?

McAllister put on his monocle to look at his pocket watch.

"You're running out of time and I'm running out of

patience," he said. "I assure you, if you don't hand over the Code in the next few minutes, it won't be *my* blood that's boiling."

Rick and Oliver exchanged looks.

Rick's said: *Don't you dare tell him.*

Oliver's said: *Don't you dare think I'd even consider telling him.*

Rick leaned back on the bars of his cage, satisfied.

He remembered the first time he and Oliver had met. They'd both been sent to Mrs. Lindstrom's Finishing School for Youth of Particularly Good Manners, and for their first three months there, they'd had no idea it was really a front for Mrs. Lindstrom's Adventurers Academy. So their first encounter hadn't been at fencing practice or on the camouflage course. No, their friendship began with a dodgeball incident.

Both Rick and Oliver had thought it a little strange that a Finishing School for Youth of Particularly Good Manners would spend so much time on dodgeball. (Later, they'd see it was part of the testing mechanism that separated future Adventurers from future non-Adventurers.)

A student named Agnes Grue had taken a particularly unholy shot at a student named Dieter Diatrix. Later, Agnes would swear she hadn't been aiming at Dieter's head, but the results were incontestable: Not only had the dodgeball slammed into Dieter's face, but it had somehow become completely ensnarled by his braces. He cried out for help, and received a mouthful of red rubber in response.

It was a mess.

A brawl broke out between Agnes's allies and Dieter's defenders—Rick and Oliver were the only students in the gymnasium who remained neutral. As gym clothes were yanked and more than one head of hair was pulled, Rick and Oliver quietly made their way to Dieter, who was in quite a state. Without needing to say a word, Rick and Oliver decided on a course of action: As Rick kept Dieter from asphyxiating, Oliver determinedly disentangled the rubber from the wire, without even needing to deflate the ball. Within a minute, Dieter was freed. The teacher, busy disentangling the brawl, didn't even notice until Oliver passed the ball back to her.

After the ball had been returned, Oliver walked over to where Rick was leaning against a gymnasium wall.

"Excellent work," he told Rick. "I'm Oliver."

"Your work was likewise excellent," Rick replied. "I'm Rick."

Rick's parents had perished only four months before. Oliver's own origins were shrouded in mystery. Neither Rick nor Oliver had realized how badly they'd needed a friend until their connection had been made.

It was impossible for Rick to imagine a life without Oliver. They had become Adventurers together, and had learned the world together.

Now, alas, they would be boiled together.

But not without a fight. Rick might not have been able to

remember facts and figures, but he was very good at calculations. And Oliver? Well, Oliver was good at understanding what Rick was calculating.

They sent each other another round of looks.

Rick's said: *Do you understand what we're about to do?*

Oliver's said: *I can't wait.*

On a silent count of two, both boys lunged from one side of their respective cages to the other. In response, Rick's cage went swinging toward Oliver's, and Oliver's went swinging toward Rick's. The second time they did this, the cages clanged together. The third time, Rick and Oliver reached out and Oliver's left hand caught Rick's right hand. Then, with their free hands, they began to pick each other's locks.

"No!" McAllister cried, motioning to his henchmen, who started to lower the cages into the boiling geyser.

"Yes!" Melody cried out, revving the motor of the cycle she'd kept in the shadows. Using McAllister's platform as a ramp, she launched herself into the air. The cage doors sprang open and Rick and Oliver pushed the cages apart to give Melody an opening just as the geyser began to erupt. . . .

4

Mom let me take the bus to school the next day.

"I have an appointment with Principal Woodson and a few of the other mothers at eleven," she told me.

I tried to keep eating my cereal as if everything were normal, as if she were telling me about a work meeting or a trip to the nail salon.

When I got on the bus, Allison waved me over. She'd saved me a seat next to her.

"Hey," I said.

She waited until I'd sat down, and then she said, "Please don't take this the wrong way . . . but I think your mom has finally lost her mind."

In response, I could only manage to gulp out a simple "What?"

Allison studied me. "Do you really not know? Your mom has been calling all the other moms, telling them that Mr. Howe is trying to turn us all gay."

This time, my "WHAT?!" was genuine.

Allison continued. "Well, not all the moms. She didn't dare call my mom. But my mom found out anyway, because moms talk. And your mom is telling everyone the book we're reading is about two boys who fall in love and run off with each other in the end. And she says the school should not be 'promoting such ideas.' I think that's a direct quote. According to Tarah's mom, who told my mom."

I looked over to the seat next to us and saw Tarah James, Olivia Parker, and Anna Cho all leaning over a book, feverishly reading and flipping pages.

"That's my copy," Allison said. "I know we were supposed to leave them at home, but I couldn't resist."

I also had my library copy in my bag—there was no way I was going to leave it alone in the house when my mom was there. I was so worried I'd fall asleep reading it last night that I only made it to chapter five before putting it safely away.

Allison didn't have the same worries in her house.

"I finished it last night," she told me. "It's not, like, a masterpiece. But it's fun. And it doesn't really matter whether Rick and Oliver end up as a couple or not. That's definitely not the point of the story. If Mr. Howe was straight, your mom probably wouldn't have said a thing."

I didn't know what to say to that. I knew Mr. Howe had a husband but wasn't sure how my mom would know that. It wasn't like I'd told her.

I could remember the one time I'd been watching TV and

had this show about high school on. I hadn't even noticed my mom was in the room until the two gay boyfriends on the show were flirting with each other in the halls, and Mom asked me, "What show is this?" I told her, and she shook her head and said, "I'd like you to watch something else." She didn't tell me that what I'd seen was wrong, and she didn't yell at me or anything for watching it, but the line was drawn, the message clear: *You are not ready for this.* There was no point in arguing.

Allison must have seen my distress, thinking about my mom saying something about Mr. Howe, because she told me, "Don't worry. My mom is sure Principal Woodson will show some spine. My parents and some of their friends have an appointment with her today."

"What time?" I asked.

"Noon, I think."

I hoped Principal Woodson knew to get my mom and her squad out of the way before Allison's mom and *her* squad arrived.

Next to me, Tarah closed Allison's copy of *The Adventurers* and passed it to the boys in the seat in front of her. The boys immediately turned to the back of the book and started reading.

Our friend Sean wasn't on our bus, but he was eager to talk as soon as we got into class. The door was open, but Mr. Howe was nowhere in sight. I tried not to be worried about that.

The first words out of Sean's mouth were "Did you read the end?"

Allison and I both said we had.

"I don't get it," Sean said, genuinely confused. "It doesn't say they're gay at all. They're just two guys going on adventures. Like Batman and Robin."

Allison gave him a look.

"What?" Sean asked.

"Batman and Robin. Didn't you ever think that maybe . . ."

"Okay, okay," Sean said. "Then like . . . Iron Man and Hulk."

Allison gave him the same look, telling him she definitely thought it was possible Iron Man and the Hulk were more than friends.

"Stop it!" Sean laughed. "The Hulk is *not* Tony Stark's type."

"Fair," Allison conceded.

I found the whole conversation very strange, if only because my mom had caused it.

There was some turning of heads when someone walked into the room. I followed that turn of heads to see Kira coming in. I'd honestly forgotten that she had two moms. There were a few kids in our school with two moms or two dads or parents who just wanted to be called parents, so it wasn't a big deal. But the current conversation made it a little more of a big deal.

She walked right over to us. Partly, I'm sure, because her desk was near mine. But partly so she could say to me, "Well, I guess now I know why you didn't have your book yesterday."

"Sorry," I told her.

"You don't need to apologize," Allison said. When Kira didn't look convinced, Allison continued. "He doesn't! It's not his fault his mom is doing this. I'm assuming, Donovan, you didn't read the book and go running to her, telling her it was doing bad things to you?"

"Um, no," I said. "She picked it up and started reading it while I was watching TV."

"You see?" Allison said.

Kira sighed. "Okay. I get that. But still, I can't believe we're having this conversation. My moms are *not* happy that suddenly someone's trying to ban a queer book in my class."

At that moment, the bell rang and Mr. Howe walked in the door.

He didn't look happy, either.

"All right, everyone . . . sit yourselves down," he said. When we were all quiet, he continued. "I'm guessing that by now you know that some parents have raised questions about my choice of reading material. I have to tell you, when I assigned the book to you, I never in a million years thought there was anything in it that would cause an objection. And having given it some more thought, I still feel there is nothing in it that's wrong to teach in this class.

But in the end, it's not my opinion that matters the most. Nor is it any single parent's opinion that matters the most. Our school system has a procedure for book challenges, and the principal has assured me that it will be followed here."

He took a deep breath, then looked as many of us in the eye as he could. "I've been instructed to collect your books for now. I've let Principal Woodson know that you weren't supposed to bring them to class today, and that since it's Friday, we probably won't be able to collect them until Monday. She understood. Is there anyone who has a copy they'd like to turn in now?"

Kids started looking around the room, wondering who'd volunteer. I turned to Allison, but she was looking around at other people, as if she didn't have a copy in her bag.

"No one?" Mr. Howe said. Then he smiled. "Figures this would be the first time you all followed my instructions."

Luther Haines raised his hand and started waving for Mr. Howe's attention.

"Yes, Luther?" Mr. Howe said.

"Rick and Oliver aren't gay, right?" Luther blurted out. "I mean, my dad said it's a gay book and it isn't really, is it?"

The smile drained from Mr. Howe's face, and now he just looked sad.

"We're not going to have this conversation now, Luther. I'm hoping that we'll continue reading the book in class, and then when we get to the end, we can talk about whatever you'd like. But I want to make this very clear to all of you: It doesn't matter how you identify Rick or Oliver, or what you think their relationship is or ultimately will be. If we're going to defend this book—and I promise you, I plan on defending this book—the proper line of defense is not 'But they're not gay!' Because that implies that there would be a legitimate problem if they *were* gay. The proper defense is 'It doesn't matter if they're gay. The characters can be whoever they are.' And I know some of you might think I'm saying that because I myself am gay. But I am not saying this as a gay man, or as a gay teacher. I'm saying this as a human being who believes that all human beings should be treated with respect."

I thought there'd be nervous giggles. Maybe some jokes. Or guys like Luther being uncomfortable. But instead there was silence—at least until Allison yelled out, "You tell 'em, Mr. Howe!" and Kira and a few other kids started clapping. I started clapping too, even though I saw some people looking over to me, expecting me not to clap, since my mom had started it all.

Mr. Howe nodded at us, then turned around so we couldn't see the rest of his reaction. He took a few more deep breaths before turning back to us and saying, "Okay, enough of that. Let's do some math."

My mother assumed I didn't know anything. Over dinner she told me and my dad that she'd had a good meeting with Principal Woodson, but that was all she said. Although I was sure that Allison was asking her mom millions of questions about how *her* meeting had gone, I didn't ask a thing. Because if I asked my mom why she was doing this, then it would become clear that I knew what she was doing. And as far as my dad was concerned . . . as usual, he wanted to keep everyone happy. At the dinner table, he used phrases like "That's good" and "Fantastic" as if they were punctuation marks to my mother's sentences. He always seemed interested in what my mother was saying, but never had much to add to it.

I was glad it was a Friday, because the weekend gave me a lot of secret reading time, so I could read *The Adventurers* cover to cover . . . even if the covers weren't the right ones. Afraid that my parents would surprise me in my room, I'd taken the jacket from a copy of *The Lion, the Witch and the Wardrobe* on my shelf and had dressed *The Adventurers* up in that. I knew my parents liked Narnia—we'd watched all the movies together—so if they opened my door and asked me what I was doing, I could simply hold up the book and they'd be satisfied. Or so I hoped. Luckily, they left me alone in my room for a lot of the weekend. My father gardened. My mother talked to people on the phone. My room was my only-child fortress.

When Monday morning came, I put the book back in

its safe place under my bed . . . and prepared to talk to my friends about it. Since they all had to turn in their copies to Mr. Howe, I was sure most of them had tried to read it as quickly as possible, to know why it was being pulled out of their hands.

I honestly didn't see what the fuss was about.

But nobody was asking me.

four

Over the next week, Gideon's days changed. It wasn't that school was less boring—it was just that Gideon now had Roberto to look forward to.

On the day after the copies of *Harriet the Spy* were passed out, Ms. June gave each two-person group a notebook to share.

"This is *not* so you can spy," she reminded the class. "Every week or so, I'll give you an assignment. The first assignment is simple: I would like you to each share five things your group partner might not know about you. Do it one at a time—one of you starts, then you pass the notebook and the other person writes one, and you go back and forth until you each do five. But it has to be something the other person doesn't already know about you."

Gideon could see that a lot of his friends in the class weren't happy about this assignment. Joelle and Tucker had immediately chosen each other as partners, and now they looked concerned—they already knew *plenty* about each other, so finding five things each was going to be hard.

With Gideon and Roberto, though, it could be anything. Roberto understood this, too, because when Ms. June handed him the notebook, he turned to Gideon and said, "Good thing we don't really know each other, right?"

"Totally," Gideon agreed.

"Do you want to go first?" Roberto asked.

"Nah. You have the notebook. You start."

Roberto grinned and immediately began to write. But it wasn't until the end of the day that he passed the notebook to Gideon.

"Your turn," he said.

Gideon wanted to open it right away . . . but not while Roberto was looking. Or in the same room. Gideon hadn't read that far in *Harriet the Spy,* but he figured the notebook was supposed to be a private thing. So he waited until he was back home, back in his room, to read what Roberto had written:

I was born in Miami, where my abuela and abuelo (my grandparents on my mom's side) still live. When I was two, we moved to Mexico City to live with my other abuela and abuelo, but when I was four, we moved back to Miami. We still go down to Mexico City every Christmas. We moved here to Virginia because my dad got a really great job, but he promised I'm still going to spend part of the summer in Miami. It's weird for me because we usually have lots of tías and tíos and primos and primas around, but here the only family is me, my mom, and my dad. I am trying to get my parents to get us a dog instead of cousins, but so far they say no.

This felt like more than one thing to Gideon, but he didn't mind finding out so much all at once. He figured he should write back and tell Roberto that he'd lived in the same place his whole life—but Roberto probably already assumed that. And also, Gideon didn't consider it to be that interesting.

"What'll I do?" Gideon asked Samson. He knew Samson wouldn't reply (*because he knew turtles couldn't talk). But even the non-reply helped get Gideon to an answer.

I like turtles.
I really like turtles.

Gideon paused for a quick count.

I have 84 turtles in my collection. 83 of them are not real turtles. But Samson is a real turtle. He lives in my room.

I try to find turtles wherever I go. I got a turtle in New York City and a turtle in Santa Fe. My grandma gave me a glass turtle she got in Copenhagen, Denmark. She didn't mail it to me because she didn't want it to break, so I didn't get it until she visited. Sometimes when the light from the window hits its shell, it makes a rainbow. It might be my favorite turtle besides Samson.

I don't think I'd like having a dog as much as I like having a turtle. But I hope you get a dog if you want a dog.

Gideon closed the notebook and thought he'd made a good start. Not that many kids in school knew about his turtle collection—just the friends who'd been over to his house.

It was only after Gideon handed the notebook back to Roberto that he began to worry that Roberto would find what he'd written silly . . . or babyish . . . or boring. Throughout the day, Gideon saw Roberto take the notebook out and write in it. But even from the seat behind him, Gideon couldn't tell what he was writing. He tried to distract himself, debating whether Ms. June was wearing the same dress she'd worn last Wednesday or last Tuesday. Then he tried to make new words of six letters or longer from *Founding Fathers* written on the board.

haunts

reading

farthing

fountain

When Roberto finally passed him the notebook after lunch, it was with a smile. Gideon knew he wouldn't last until the end of the day, so when Roberto's back was turned again and Ms. June was deep into a lesson on molecules, he opened up the notebook.

In it, Roberto had written:

I like turtles too.

Surrounding the sentence, he had drawn lots of turtles. No two were the same. Some were realistic turtles. Some were cartoon turtles. One was a rainbow turtle.

Gideon didn't need to count them to know there were eighty-four total.

Then he counted them. And there were eighty-four total.

His joy at finding so many turtles waiting for him lasted for a few minutes. Then he started to stress out. How could he respond to this? There was no way he could draw eighty-four dogs.

At this point, Ms. June saw that he had the notebook out. She didn't need to say a word—she just locked eyes for a moment with Gideon and he knew he had to put it away and focus on molecules.

At the end of the day, he put the notebook in his book bag and hoped Samson would be able to help him again. On his way out of class, he asked his friend Mia what she'd written to her partner (Isaac) and she said she'd told him a story about the time her cousin sat on her birthday cake. (*Gideon already knew this story, but apparently Isaac didn't.) As he started to walk the few blocks home, he tried to think of something hilarious that had happened to him on a birthday. Half a block into the walk, he felt someone come alongside him. He turned his head and found Roberto there.

"So why do you like turtles so much?" Roberto asked. His tone was casual, as if they walked home together every day.

"Um . . . ," Gideon replied. "I guess I like how they carry their home with them. It's not like they have a whole house, but it's like they take their room with them. If they're tired, they can just pull into their shell and go to sleep. The shells are really cool." Gideon thought about it some more. "And maybe I also like them because they're slow. A turtle's never going to jump out at you. It might snap at you, but it's never going to attack you in a way that'll really hurt. You don't need to walk them or worry about them running away. Also, they can live in water and on land, which means that a turtle probably gets to see more of the world than we do."

"I love it," Roberto said.

Gideon blushed.

Then Roberto asked, "So when do I get to meet Samson?"

And Gideon, uncertain, answered, "Now?"

"Sure!" Roberto said. "Do you live nearby? I just have to be home by four for my piano lesson."

"I live two blocks down that way," Gideon said.

"Nice! I live three blocks down *that* way. I think."

It felt like a miracle to Gideon, that they lived so close together. (*In reality, the town wasn't very big.)

Gideon was not by nature a rule-breaker. But he did make exceptions when he felt the rules were wrong. For example, his parents did not allow him to have friends over when they weren't at home. Since they worked until five or six every day, this meant that Gideon was basically not allowed to have any friends over except on weekends. Which wasn't at all fair.

In breaking this particular rule at this particular time, Gideon was careful. When he and Roberto went to the kitchen to get a snack, he made sure they didn't pick the same snack, because his mother was much more likely to notice two of the same thing missing than one each of two separate things. He also left the door from the garage open, because when the door from the garage was open, the whole house could hear when someone came home.

When they got to his room to meet Samson, Gideon felt overwhelmed. Roberto immediately started looking around, taking everything in, and Gideon thought to himself that now he'd have far fewer things to put in the notebook, because Roberto was getting to know him much more in five minutes than he would have from any number of pages of Gideon's writing.

The first destination was the terrarium. As Gideon carefully removed the lid and asked Samson about his day, Roberto looked at the other eighty-three turtles arrayed on their shelves.

"Do they all have names?" he asked. "All my stuffed animals have names."

Gideon was surprised by the question. It hadn't even occurred to him to give the turtles names (*besides Samson). Each of them meant something to him individually, and each had a story it carried with it. But not names. They were the blue marble one, the one with too much makeup, the one with the Empire State Building on its shell. And so forth.

"Only Samson has a name," Gideon confessed. Then he thought for a second about what Roberto had said and added, "How many stuffed animals do you have?"

"A lot," Roberto answered. "Eighty-four."

Then he smiled and asked to be introduced to Samson.

Gideon removed the turtle from the terrarium and held him up so he was eye-to-eye with Roberto.

"Samson, this is Roberto. Roberto, Samson."

The smile hadn't left Roberto's face. "It's very nice to meet you, Samson," he said.

Samson didn't reply. (*Because he's a turtle.) But he didn't pull back into his shell, which he often did when meeting new people.

"He likes you." Gideon was confident he could speak on Samson's behalf.

He put Samson down, and the two boys sat on the rug and played with him for a bit. Roberto saw Gideon's copy of *Harriet the Spy* on the floor next to the bed. He reached over and picked it up, to see where the bookmark was placed.

"I'm not that far," Gideon admitted, self-conscious again. "Only the first three chapters."

"You haven't met my favorite character, then," Roberto said.

"Who's that?" Gideon asked.

"You'll see," Roberto teased. Then he examined the piece of paper Gideon was using as a bookmark. On it were the words:

I see art
There's a hit
Yet I spare
Tipsy heart
The heir's party

"What's this?" Roberto asked.

"Oh. It's stupid. Just something I do."

Gideon was about to explain further, but then Roberto said, "You rearrange the letters, right? That's cool. You used all the letters for the last one, didn't you?"

"Yeah. *The heir's party* is the only phrase I've found so far that has all the letters from *Harriet the Spy*."

"We'll have to figure out some more!"

Gideon was thrilled by this news.

"Yeah, we'll have to," he said.

Then, for the rest of the time that Roberto could stay, they sat on the floor with Samson and tried.

CHAPTER ELEVEN:
INTO THE WOODS

"It wasn't your fault that McAllister got away," Rick assured Oliver.

Oliver knew that Rick was factually correct. It didn't feel that way, though.

Melody had set the bear trap with such precision. But Oliver had gotten too close, and when he'd dodged it, McAllister had seen the dodge and steered clear—straight to safety.

"Seriously," Melody said, bringing over some firewood, "don't sweat it."

Oliver knew that his friends didn't keep track of the times he messed up. He kept track for them. The time he slipped on the Eiffel Tower. The time he got Diet Pepsi for the diplomat instead of Diet Coke and threw off the whole password. The time he hadn't spotted the tracker on his bicycle until he was halfway toward their safe house. The time he'd thought the English project was due on Thursday when it was really due on Wednesday, and he and Rick had needed to ask a secret service agent to stop at a bookstore on the way to the airport . . .

Oops. Rick was saying his name.

"What?" Oliver asked.

Rick shook his head. "Lost you to the inventory system again, didn't we? It's a drag to see you fall into that pit."

Oliver added to the list: *The time I was a real drag after McAllister got away from us.*

"Look," Rick said, "it isn't every day that we get to toast marshmallows by a campfire in the middle of the wilderness."

"We don't have marshmallows." Oliver sulked. "And the fire has to be kept low so we're not spotted."

"Fine!" Rick cried, standing up. "I will go get us some marshmallows!" Then, before Oliver could say another word, he stormed off.

Rick knew full well that what he'd just said didn't make much sense. They were in the middle of the wilderness. Marshmallows did not grow on trees. And yet, here he was, skulking off into the woods. Because this was what often happened—when Oliver sulked, Rick skulked. Rick didn't know any other way to handle it. While he was off, Oliver would begin the unsulking process. And then when Rick got back, Rick would do something to complete the process, like make a joke.

In this particular case, he desperately wanted to find something in the woods that looked like a marshmallow. Or even something that could make a good marshmallow pun. Like marsh grass. If he could find some marsh grass and bend it into the shape of a duck, he could present it to Oliver as a marshmallard. Oliver would laugh and, together with Melody, they'd toast marshmallards over the fire.

Did it matter that there wasn't any marsh grass in this area? Not at all. Rick didn't have any idea what marsh grass looked like, so he assumed Oliver didn't either. Any old grass that was long enough to shape into a duck would do.

Rick was careful not to venture too far into the woods—in the rush of his skulking, he'd forgotten to bring a flashlight, and the moon was laying a ghostly glare over the forest. He had leaned over to test out some grass around a boulder when he felt a presence on the other side of the boulder.

He looked up . . . and found himself staring at a bear, no more than ten feet away.

Rick knew that with grizzly bears, you were supposed to slowly edge back and play dead if they attacked. With black bears, you were supposed to hold your ground and scare them.

It also helped to carry bear spray.

Rick was not carrying bear spray.

Nor could he tell in the dark whether this was a grizzly bear or a black bear.

His first impulse was to scream. Since bears are afraid of sudden, loud noises, he decided to go for it.

"BEAR!" he yelled in the loudest voice he could muster. "BEAEAEAEAEAR!"

The bear decided to yell back.

It came out as an angry roar.

Stand your ground, Rick thought.

RUN! he also thought.

And: *No, remember you're not supposed to run!*

It was a boy-and-bear standoff . . .

. . . until suddenly there was a clamor from behind Rick. A monstrous cacophony that made even the trees shake.

CLANG! CLANG! CLANG!

The bear turned and ran.

Rick wanted to follow . . . until Oliver and Melody ran up to him, pots and pans from the RV in hand. They'd crashed them together to make as much noise as possible.

Oliver looked around. "Well, the good news is, I don't see any more bears."

"And the bad news?" Rick asked, noticing that the sulking had been cured by a need for action.

Oliver nodded to Melody, who said, "The bad news is that everyone in a twenty-mile radius probably just heard us."

It was time to get out of there.

5

Mr. Howe's classroom was very crowded on Monday morning.

Principal Woodson was there at the front of the room, alongside Mr. Howe and Ms. Guy. Parents were there, too. Some parents wanted to turn in their child's copy of *The Adventurers* themselves, as if they didn't trust their child to let go of it when asked. I had no doubt my mom would have been one of them, if she hadn't already confiscated mine and turned it in. Luckily this meant there wasn't any need for her to be present.

There were other parents, like Mr. and Mrs. Fitzhugh (Allison's mom and dad) and Mrs. and Mrs. Pausacker (Kira's moms), who were explaining that they were *not* turning in their child's copy of the book, because they didn't believe that parents like my mom should have the power to choose what their own children read or didn't read.

Principal Woodson looked overwhelmed. Mr. Howe

looked sad. Ms. Guy reminded everyone of the proper procedure for a book challenge in our school system. Kira's moms
held hands as one of them pressed Principal Woodson to say
what, exactly, was being objected to. None of the other parents, the ones who'd brought in their kids' books, wanted
to say it.

It was an interesting scene, for sure.

But some of us were in the back of the class, focused on
something else.

"It doesn't matter whether they are or not . . . but Rick
and Oliver are definitely gay," Allison said.

"It's not *definite*," Sean said. His parents had let him
bring back the book himself.

"I wasn't sure at first," Luther said. "But, yeah, by the
end—so gay."

"But what about Melody?" Patience asked. "Don't you
think they're both crushing on Melody?"

"There's a difference between flirting and crushing,"
Kira said.

"I think Rick loves her," Tarah said quietly.

"I think Rick loves Oliver," Amelia countered.

"I think the point of the book is that the Adventurers
need to stop McAllister from unleashing his evil on the world
through the Doomsday Code," Jeffrey put in. "I don't think
Rick and Oliver are in love or not in love. I think they're
friends and, most importantly, Adventurers. You guys just
don't understand the Adventurers' mission *at all*."

Allison and some others looked skeptical, so I said, "C'mon—you have to admit, Jeffrey has a point. If this were a week ago, we'd all be talking about the action scenes. And yes, Patience, maybe about which of the boys Melody liked more. The only reason we're talking about whether or not Rick and Oliver are gay is because we were told that was a part of it before we had a chance to read it."

I didn't even realize the trap I'd walked into until Curtis said, "Yeah, Donovan. And whose fault is that? Who decided to pull the books out of our hands before any of us had a chance to read it?"

"That's not fair," Allison said. "It's not his fault that his mom . . . did what she did."

Curtis looked me in the eye. "How do we know it wasn't you who went crying to your mommy, complaining that the book was going to make him gay?"

"That's not what happened," I said quickly. "She took it off the kitchen counter and read the ending while I was watching TV."

Curtis looked satisfied by this explanation. Then he said, "Good. Because I happen to know that the author of this book must be gay, and Rick and Oliver must be gay too. Because I'm gay, and I know what he's talking about."

This was news to all of us.

"Oh wow," Patience said.

"That's awesome," Kira said.

"Very cool," Jeffrey added.

Luther, who was one of Curtis's best friends, looked surprised. "Dude," he said, "I had no idea."

Ron, another of Curtis's best friends, laughed and said, "Really?"

He hugged Curtis, and then Luther piled on, followed by Allison and Sean. That got the attention of the adults in the front of the room.

"What's going on?" Principal Woodson asked.

Someone said, "Nothing." And a couple more kids also said, "Nothing." And when the hug was over, Curtis grinned and said, "We're talking about the book. And how cool it is that Rick and Oliver are gay."

A couple kids laughed at that . . . and a few others started to cheer. Like a big hooray for the fact that Rick and Oliver were gay. When what we really meant, of course, was a big hooray for the fact that Curtis was gay. And I say *we* here because I was definitely one of the kids cheering.

Principal Woodson smiled—and at that moment I thought, *Oh, she's on our side after all.*

"All right," she said, loud enough for everyone in the classroom to hear. "I think we've disrupted this class long enough. If you have any copies of the book you'd like to deposit here on the table, to remain here pending the official review of the book challenge, please do so now. I suggest any parents who would like to discuss this with me further head down to the lounge next to my office. Mr. Howe, you have a very spirited group in this class—how refreshing to see youth so impassioned about literature."

A lot of the parents loved that line, and a few of them clearly didn't. I was really glad my mom wasn't in the room . . . though I was sure she'd hear about it later.

Once everyone else had left the room, Mr. Howe called for some order. Kids were still patting Curtis on the back and giving him thumbs-up signs.

"What's going on?" Mr. Howe asked in Curtis's general direction.

"I'm gay, Mr. Howe," Curtis replied.

This was *not* the answer Mr. Howe was expecting, but he took it in stride.

"I'm gay too," he said. "Feels good to say it out loud, doesn't it?"

Curtis smiled. "It does, Mr. Howe."

"Okay, then," Mr. Howe said. "If any of you want to talk about this some more, you know where to find me. But for now, it's time for us to hear a few current events reports."

"But what about Rick and Oliver?" Allison asked. "Aren't we going to talk about Rick and Oliver?"

"Not right now," Mr. Howe said. "As long as the books remain on this table, that means our discussion of the book is on pause. As Ms. Guy noted, there is a procedure in place for book challenges, and we are going to follow it. This week the review committee, which includes Principal Woodson and Ms. Guy, will read the book. Next Monday they will meet to discuss it, and on Wednesday they will provide their findings in an open school board meeting where a decision will be made, hopefully in line with the committee's recommendation. I imagine many of your parents will be at that meeting."

"Can kids come too?" Allison asked, without waiting to be called on.

"I believe so," Mr. Howe said. Then he added, "But you'll have to ask your parents. Are there any other questions before we move on?"

"Has anyone contacted the author? Mr. Bright?" Patience asked.

Mr. Howe looked momentarily surprised by the question. Then he said, "I'm not sure. I know Ms. Guy has been in touch with the National Coalition Against Censorship, an organization that helps defend free speech, and the American Library Association. But none of us have been in touch with Mr. Bright directly."

"We should write to him!" Allison said. "We don't know anything about him."

"Yeah," Luther agreed. "He'll know if Rick and Oliver are gay."

Mr. Howe held up a hand. "While the meaning of a book may be informed by the author's intentions, it isn't defined by them. Meaning comes from the combination of what the author puts in and what the reader takes out. And, I'll remind you, it doesn't matter whether Rick and Oliver are romantically in love or in love as friends—either is completely acceptable for a story taught in this classroom."

There was wild agreement from us students about this, with more than a few glances thrown Curtis's way. Mr. Howe began the current events reports, calling on Allison to start. We all pretended to listen . . . but I could tell that, like me, most of us were still thinking about Rick and Oliver and the mysterious Mr. Bright.

"We have to write to him," Allison said as soon as we were gathered at recess, out of hearing range of the recess supervisor. "There has to be a way to email G. R. Bright."

"That's not his real name, you know," Kira said. "It's there in his bio."

This was true. G. R. Bright's "About the Author" read:

> G. R. Bright is the pen name for a writer who
> lives outside Denver with his family. He is
> also the author of a number of books of adult
> nonfiction under his real name, none of which
> would be of any interest to readers of this novel.
> He is currently working on his second novel and
> is afraid he has jinxed himself to never finish it
> by admitting it in this bio. For not that much
> more information about G. R. Bright, you can
> check out the website below.

"His website probably has an email address," Sean offered.

Since phones were strictly forbidden during recess, none of us could check.

"I think Donovan should write to him," Luther said. "Since he's the best writer in our class *and* because his mom started it all."

I thought someone would disagree. But instead everyone looked at me for a response.

"Fine," I said. "I'll do it."

"I can look up interviews with him," Kira said.

"I'll see if he has any YouTube videos," Patience offered.

It was a plan. Sort of. We had no idea whether it would lead to any answers, or if those answers would help Mr. Howe at all. But it was something to do instead of sitting and waiting for the grown-ups to decide.

I had a computer class after school at the Y, and my dad picked me up when it was through.

"How was school today?" he asked once we'd been driving for a minute or two and I'd been silent.

"Okay," I said.

"What did you do?"

I didn't really think he wanted me to give details, so I just said, "I did . . . *school*."

He sighed. "I mean . . . are the kids being mean to you?"

At first I didn't get it. Then I did.

"Because of what Mom's doing?"

"That's not the way I'd say it . . . but yes."

"The kids are fine. But I don't understand why Mom is doing it. It doesn't make any sense to me."

Dad sighed again. "Your mother cares a lot about you. This is coming from a caring place."

"Maybe if she cared about me she wouldn't be attacking my favorite teacher or a good book."

Now Dad looked irritated. I remembered too late that my parents didn't know I'd actually read the book.

Lucky for me, that wasn't the part of the sentence that had irritated him.

"Your mother and all the other parents are not *attacking* anyone or anything. Your mother simply disagrees with your teacher's choice of reading material, which is her right to do as a parent. And, again, she is doing that because she cares about you, and because that book may contain things that you are not ready to read at your age. I don't think she'd have any objection to you reading it in high school. Just not now."

I honestly wanted to laugh. But then I would have had to explain why I was laughing, which I didn't think would go over very well. And I also couldn't say, *There's nothing in that book that's bad for me, or that I'm not ready for.* Because then he'd *really* know I'd read the book.

So I just stayed quiet. And he stayed quiet. And we didn't talk about it again for the rest of the ride home.

Dad went into his home office after we got inside, and I went to my room to do homework. But of course the biggest assignment I had was to try to contact Bright . . . which was going to be hard to do while my parents were around. My mom conducted "spot checks" on my phone—she understood why I had to have one, but the condition was that she could ask for it at any time to see who I'd been calling or what I'd been looking up on the internet.

They didn't check my computer history as much. But the rule was that if I was on my laptop in my room, I had to keep the door open. They didn't want me going onto sites they didn't approve of . . . even though they'd never actually told me what those sites were.

I had to imagine that Bright's website counted as one of them right now.

I crept by the door to my dad's office, and it sounded like he was on the phone. That was a good sign. His work calls were usually long, and Mom wouldn't be home for another half hour at least.

As soon as the screen welcomed me, I typed in Bright's website address. There weren't any photos of him, just a drawing. I couldn't really tell how old he was—just that he wore glasses.

There was a page called "Frequently Asked Questions." Stuff like did he have a dog (no), did he ever go on adventures (yes, but without bad guys chasing him), what was his favorite color (green). I'd been hoping people had frequently asked about Rick and Oliver, but it didn't look like they had.

There was a button that said Contact. At first, I hesitated to click it, as if clicking it would dial his phone and suddenly I'd be talking to him. I looked instead at the page for *The Adventurers,* hoping I'd find some answers there. But all I got were some reviews, most of which called Rick and Oliver "friends" or "chums." The book description on the page also called them "friends"—was that my answer? I could see myself printing out this page and waving it around in class tomorrow, proclaiming to everyone that Rick and Oliver were friends, that's all. Then my mother would have to say she was wrong, and the whole challenge would be canceled, and we could all go back to reading the book.

I liked the idea of that.

But then I imagined going into class, sharing my discovery . . . and having Mr. Howe point out that Rick and Oliver could be friends *and* gay. Mr. Howe would say that he was friends with his husband. Kira would point out that her moms were friends. And who knew what Curtis would say?

I sighed, took a deep breath, and clicked on Contact.

No phone was dialed. No chat box popped up. Instead, there was an email address.

At that moment, I heard footsteps in the hall, followed by my dad calling my name and telling me Mom was home.

I quickly closed the window on the computer and loaded

up some homework. By the time my father was in my doorway, saying maybe we'd go out to dinner tonight, everything was safe.

I hadn't been caught.

And I also hadn't had to think of what I was going to say to G. R. Bright.

five

Over the course of the week, Gideon and Roberto continued to pass the notebook back and forth, sharing new facts about themselves.

I sometimes wake up in the middle of the night and read while my parents are asleep (*Gideon wrote).

Just like Harriet! (*Roberto replied, then added:) In third grade, the kids liked to play weddings at recess and I didn't want to marry anyone so I told them I would be the priest and lead the ceremony. If I hadn't volunteered for that, I probably would have had to marry this girl named Megan. That wouldn't have worked out.

The only wedding I've ever been to was Aunt Hannah's. It was her third marriage and I had the most fun because I hadn't been to the other two. I was the ring bearer. The guy she married smelled like Doritos. They aren't married anymore. (*Gideon)

Do you know what you want to be when you grow up? I think I want to be a scientist or maybe someone who makes buildings. But I could also be a nurse. (*Roberto)

When I grow up I am going to be a turtle trainer. Because I love turtles and training them is not a lot of work at all, because there aren't many things you can train them to do. I looked it up in the library. (*Gideon, of course)

Gideon asked his parents if he could invite his new friend to come over at some point during the weekend. When they said yes, Gideon was excited to tell Roberto the news. Roberto also seemed excited.

"Just remember to pretend like you've never been there before," Gideon said.

"Why?" Roberto looked a mix of offended and confused.

"Oh!" Gideon exclaimed. He had forgotten to tell Roberto about the no-friends-over-during-the-week rule. Once Gideon explained, Roberto looked much less offended and much less confused.

"Wow," Roberto said. "You broke the rules for me!"

"And once you start, it's hard to stop. Guess we'll just have to find new ones to break," Gideon responded.

A mischievous gleam sparkled from Roberto's eyes. "I guess so," he said. Then Ms. June called the class to order, and the conversation had to stop there. For now.

Gideon spent most of Saturday reading *Harriet the Spy*, trying to figure out which character was Roberto's favorite. He also debated how much he should clean up his room, compared to the way it had been when Roberto had seen it. He was worried that if he cleaned up too much, Roberto would notice. And he was worried that if he didn't clean up at all, Roberto would also notice. As a result he tried to make his room as exactly like the last time Roberto had seen it as possible. (*Although he did also dust his turtles because Saturday was a day he usually dusted his turtles.)

By Saturday night, Gideon felt okay about Roberto coming over. By Sunday morning, he was worried again. The problem? His parents. He didn't like what they were wearing. He didn't like the questions they asked him about Roberto over breakfast. He didn't like the little slurping noises they made when they ate their cereal or the even littler slurping noises they made when they sipped their coffee. He knew that it was highly unlikely that they would be eating cereal or sipping coffee in front of Roberto, but Gideon was worried there would be other strange noises they'd make, or strange questions they'd ask, or strange requests, like Roberto having to spend some time with the whole family before he and Gideon could go off together. On Sundays when Gideon just wanted to be alone to read or play games, his mom and dad would jokingly call him Mr. Antisocial. Gideon didn't want them to call him that in front of Roberto. Or Giddy—which they hadn't called him since he was in kindergarten, but it would probably be just his luck that they'd break it back out in front of Roberto.

Gideon almost called Roberto to cancel.

Then he thought, no, that would be even worse.

He wondered why he was making such a big deal about it. He'd had friends over before. Nothing that embarrassing had ever happened, outside of his mom taking way, way too many pictures at his birthday party and forcing everyone to play pin-the-tail-on-the-donkey and fussing if they moved the furniture and exposed some dust. He didn't worry when Tucker and Joelle came over, either alone or together. They were friends. Roberto was a new friend. Therefore, he should feel the same way about Roberto as he did about them.

Only, it felt different.

He wanted Roberto's friendship in a way he didn't feel he'd wanted any of the others'.

Maybe because it felt like those other friends had always been around.

Gideon told himself that was it.

To distract himself until noon, he read *Harriet the Spy* almost to the end. He wasn't sure how he felt about Harriet. He understood her need to write things down. But he didn't understand why the things she wrote down had to be so mean. It was like she went out of her way to see only the bad things about people. That felt exhausting to Gideon.

At 11:45, he checked his room one more time, then went downstairs to wait for Roberto to show up.

"Do you want me to make you lunch?" Gideon's mom asked.

Thinking quickly, Gideon answered, "I'm going to show him Antonoff's. He hasn't been there yet."

"Oh. Okay," Mrs. White replied. "Let me get my purse. You'll come back here after, won't you? I made a fruit salad."

A fruit salad. For some reason, these words filled Gideon with dread. But he kept a smile on as his mom gave him a ten-dollar bill and told him not to spend it all on arcade games.

At 11:58, Gideon spotted Roberto striding up the front walk. He felt the impulse to run out the door and steer him away, but knew his parents were likely to follow if he did. So he let Roberto walk up and ring the doorbell, and even waited a few seconds before answering, so it wouldn't seem like he'd been standing there the whole time.

"Wow!" Roberto said as he stepped inside. "So this is

your house! It's amazing to *finally* see it. It's *exactly* like I pictured!"

Roberto then gave him a look that was a wink without the wink. Gideon winked back without actually winking. His parents were watching, after all.

Introductions were made, and Gideon was relieved when his parents weren't too embarrassing. When Mrs. White said, "I hope you have fun at Antonoff's!" Roberto didn't say, "What are you talking about?" and instead played along like it was something he and Gideon had planned together.

Gideon got them out of there as quickly as possible.

"They're nice," Roberto said once the door was closed.

"Yeah," Gideon said. (*They were, after all, nice, even if they could also be embarrassing and overly concerned about dust.) Then he asked, "Have you ever been to Antonoff's?"

Roberto shook his head, so as Gideon led them there, he explained that Antonoff's was this sandwich shop within walking distance—it was one of the only places besides school that his parents allowed him to walk to alone. It had good food, but the best part was that in the back there were two old video games (*Pac-Man* and *Asteroids*) and an even older pinball machine.

"We're going to have to buy something, because Mr. Antonoff gets really annoyed when you ask him for singles and quarters without buying something. Are you hungry?"

"I'm okay," Roberto said. "But look . . . I didn't bring any money with me. I thought we were going to be at your house."

"I've got you," Gideon said.

"Only if I can get you next time."

"Deal." Gideon liked that they were already planning a next time.

At the store, they each got some potato chips and two "freshly baked" chocolate chip cookies that made Gideon observe to Roberto that the words *hard, fake,* and *bad* were hidden in the phrase *freshly baked.*

When this caused Roberto to laugh in appreciation, Gideon felt emboldened to keep talking. He explained that *Pac-Man* and *Asteroids* were possibly his favorite video games because they didn't involve anyone getting killed, not even aliens. In *Pac-Man,* you swallowed ghosts—and ghosts were already dead, right? And in *Asteroids,* you were just blasting rocks. No harm in that.

He also admitted that pinball stressed him out.

"Pinball's more fun when it's two-player," Roberto said.

"What do you mean?" Gideon asked.

"Get some quarters and I'll show you."

Gideon fed some dollar bills into the change machine, then brought the resulting change to the pinball machine. Its theme was *Star Trek,* and the Starship *Enterprise* glowed on the headboard.

"Okay," Roberto said, "so you take that flipper and I take this flipper and we try to play together."

This meant Gideon and Roberto had to stand really close together in the middle, while Gideon used his left hand to control the left flipper and Roberto used his right hand to control the right flipper.

It was a disaster at first. Both boys were right-handed, so Gideon felt particularly awkward on the left. And it still stressed him out whenever the ball came speeding toward the bottom, the flippers the only defense preventing its escape. When the ball came down decidedly on one side or the other, they had a chance. But if it was toward the middle, they kept botching it. Gideon would tip it in or Roberto would launch his flipper a half second after Gideon's when they both needed to hit it at the same time.

By the fifth quarter spent, Gideon was ready to give up.

Roberto, however, was undaunted.

"Look," he said, putting his arm around Gideon's waist, "we have to pretend we're one body."

Gideon didn't know what he was supposed to do. If anything, having Roberto's hand there made him feel more awkward. But before he could say anything, Roberto put another quarter in and sprang the ball into action. He pressed his hip into Gideon's, and, to balance it out, Gideon found his arm moving behind Roberto's back.

"Concentrate," Roberto said.

So Gideon did. He focused on the ball. He tried not to think of what Roberto would do. Instead he just hit the flipper when the ball was coming closer. Sure enough, they fell in sync. They kept the ball in play, blasting against bumpers and doing laps across sensors that made the machine beep with pleasure.

Gideon didn't think he'd ever been this close to another person before. He didn't understand how Roberto didn't seem to notice it when all Gideon could do was notice it.

After the game was done (*with them achieving the machine's high score for the day), Roberto put his arm down so he could step away for some chips. When he came back, they went back to being side by side, hip against hip, shoulder to shoulder . . . but Roberto kept his left hand in front of him, so Gideon did the same with his right. They remained in sync even if they weren't holding each other, howling at the injustice when the ball got past them.

Eventually, Roberto proposed they move on to *Asteroids,* then *Pac-Man.* They played two-player rounds until they ran out of quarters. Gideon cursed himself for not thinking to bring more money.

"Next time," Roberto reminded him.

The promise of next time wasn't enough for Gideon. He wanted to stay here, like this, for as long as humanly possible.

But as soon as he thought that, three teenagers came along to play *Pac-Man,* and the bubble that had surrounded Gideon and Roberto popped.

"Guess we'll go back to your house?" Roberto said.

In response, Gideon asked, "Have you been to the brook?"

Once again, Roberto shook his head, and Gideon took the lead. The brook was something less than a river and more than a stream. It ran behind Antonoff's and some of the houses in the neighborhood. To get to it, you had to scramble down a steep bank. It was almost impossible to do without getting your pants dirty. Gideon decided it was worth it, and slid down with Roberto at his side.

There wasn't much to see at the brook. Just water and rocks and a few trees, with the houses looming above. There was barely a bank to walk along.

Still, Roberto said, "This is cool." And Gideon told him about how he and Tucker, when they were very little, used to think it led to a magical land. They'd even tried to send a message in a bottle once, to see if the people (*or creatures) in the magical land would write back.

"Did they?" Roberto asked, not serious.

"Nope," Gideon said.

"Or maybe they did—except that they put it in an invisible bottle, not realizing human eyes wouldn't be able to see it."

"Yeah," Gideon said. "That has to be it."

As they walked along the brook, Roberto picked up a few sticks and sent them sailing. Every now and then he'd look into the backyards above them. If you looked across the brook, you could usually see into the houses.

"Harriet would love this," Roberto observed. "A perfect place to spy. No dumbwaiters needed."

"I'm almost done with the book," Gideon said. "Tell me who your favorite character is."

"Guess."

"Sport?"

"I like Sport, especially because of all he does for his dad. But no."

"Ole Golly?"

"Too many quotes."

"Um . . . Janie?"

Roberto stopped walking. "No—I think she's a little too into blowing things up."

"So who is it?"

Roberto smiled. "The Boy with the Purple Socks. I think I'm in love with him."

So many things about this statement surprised Gideon that he genuinely couldn't come up with a response.

Roberto, though, responded as if Gideon had said something.

"I know it's silly, because we don't know that much about him. But I love that he wears purple socks. And I also love that he's the new kid in school but he's still the one leading the parade. Harriet says he's boring but that's just because she hasn't bothered to talk to him. I think he's pretty funny."

The Boy with the Purple Socks hadn't made this kind of an impression on Gideon.

The way Roberto said *I think I'm in love with him,* though—that made quite an impression.

Gideon felt the question inside him, but couldn't find the words to make the question.

So instead, he slid a little back into his shell. He looked at his watch and said it was getting late, and that they should probably make an appearance at his house before his parents started to wonder if he was ever coming home. Roberto seemed excited to go there, and remained excited even when Mr. and Mrs. White were asking him all about where he'd lived before and what street he lived on now and if he was interested in having some fruit salad. Roughly twenty berries and seven chunks of melon later, Gideon and Roberto sat in the rec room, playing some Nintendo. Gideon enjoyed it, but it wasn't like pinball.

They were playing *Super Mario,* but all Gideon could think about was the Boy with the Purple Socks.

CHAPTER SIXTEEN:
WRESTLING WITH MORE
THAN ALLIGATORS

Mrs. Lindstrom briefed Melody on McAllister's whereabouts.

"He has various hideaways around the country, as you know," Mrs. Lindstrom said. "But our informants tell us that he's bunked up in the Alligator Kingdom."

Melody shuddered.

"That place is a fortress," she observed.

Mrs. Lindstrom nodded. "It makes Fort Knox seem like a neighborhood candy store. Jacques Le Jacques is very powerful and very paranoid—a combination that leads to the highest security level possible."

"Do we smoke him out?" Melody asked. "Or do you advise that we infiltrate the place?"

Mrs. Lindstrom looked grave. "I'm not sure there's a way to get him out . . . so you're going to have to go in."

"Got it," Melody said. There was no point in arguing. An assignment was an assignment.

As soon as she was off the comm with Mrs. Lindstrom, she

loaded up the Adventurers' dossier on Jacques Le Jacques. He was a renowned alligator wrestler who'd found fame and fortune in reality TV, parlaying that fame and fortune into being elected governor of Florida for two years. He only left office after being caught using state money to construct monuments to his favorite alligators, to be placed around his fortress. His emotional press conference admitting his misdeeds caused one of Melody's favorite newspaper headlines ever: *ALLIGATOR TEARS: Embezzler Tearfully Admits to Being Governor of Florida.*

Rick and Oliver were in a good mood on returning from their grocery run—a mood entirely related to all the chips, soda, and cheese they'd purchased. The mood slipped, though, when they came into the RV and saw Melody's expression.

"We're going to have to drain the swamp," she informed them, then explained their next mission.

Rick took it in stride, but Oliver looked haunted. He quickly excused himself, saying he'd put the groceries away.

Melody knew there was a story here that she hadn't yet been told.

"What's going on?" she asked Rick.

She could see the seconds it took for Rick to remind himself that he trusted her.

"It's Florida," he said. "That's where Oliver's parents . . . abandoned him. He was found in a booth in a Denny's. Nobody saw who left him there. One of the waiters took him home and raised him until he got into the finishing school."

"That's awful."

"It's even worse. For the first few years of his life, they named him Denny."

"No."

"Yeah. Kinda hard to forget what happened that way, you know? Once he learned that wasn't his actual name, he made them change it."

"Weird."

"It actually gets weirder."

"How?"

Rick sighed. "Okay—but you can't let him know I told you."

"Of course," Melody swore.

"The only reason I'm telling you is—well, you'll figure it out soon enough. You know how sometimes they sell alligator heads? Like, small ones to use as paperweights, big ones to hang on your wall or something?"

"Is that really a thing people do?"

"In Florida, yes. Just picture it—an alligator head, its jaws intact. Glass eyes. Dried-out skin."

"Okay, I get the picture."

"Well, when Oliver was found . . . whoever left him at Denny's left him in the mouth of an alligator head."

"Whoa."

"Yeah. Pretty twisted. But the teeth hadn't been clamping on him for too long. There aren't any marks. I checked."

"How does he know this?"

Rick shook his head sadly. "People took pictures. Like, they just stood there and took pictures until that waiter saw what was happening, rushed over, and saved Oliver."

"Do you think there's some connection to Jacques Le Jacques?"

Rick shrugged, then said, "I don't think so. I mean, there are plenty of people in Florida who wrestle alligators, right? The point is, Oliver feels weird about going back to Florida. Because the kind of person who leaves a baby in an alligator's mouth in a booth at Denny's isn't likely to leave Florida."

"Should I tell Mrs. Lindstrom? Get him reassigned?"

Now Rick looked horrified. "No way. We can't do this without him. Mrs. Lindstrom knows that. She knows all of this. And Oliver is an Adventurer—he'll put his personal baggage aside for the mission. I'm sure of it."

Melody thought this sounded right, from what she knew of Oliver. Which meant that both she and Rick were surprised by Oliver's reaction when they finally went to the kitchen to talk to him about it.

"I don't get it," Oliver said, slamming a canister of frosting onto the RV's small kitchen counter. "When did being an Adventurer become about chasing down evil people? Why can't we just have a fun adventure every now and then? We're called the Adventurers. Not the Rescuers. Not the World Savers. Or the . . ."

"Bad Guy Catchers?" Rick offered.

"*Exactly!*" Oliver said, triumphant.

"But the two go hand in hand," Melody said.

Both Rick and Oliver turned to her and said, "What?"

"You can't have adventures without freedom," Melody pointed out. "And you can't have freedom if you're not willing to defend it from the people who want to take it away."

"You're not even an Adventurer," Oliver scoffed. "You talk to headquarters. You go along with us. But you refuse to join up. So how can you talk?"

"Because I don't believe you have to belong to any group to have adventures," Melody said calmly. "And I don't believe you should have to join any organization in order to have freedom."

Rick could see Oliver taking this in, and stayed silent, wondering what his friend would say next.

Oliver reached onto the kitchen counter for a bag of Hint of Lime Tostitos, popped it open, and offered it to Melody and Rick.

"Fine," he said. "I get it. We stop McAllister once and for all."

"Even if it means going to Florida?" Rick asked carefully.

Oliver nodded decisively. "Even if it means going to Florida. Let's wrestle some gators."

6

It didn't take long for the news to spread all over Sandpiper Township.

It started with all the fifth-grade parents, and then all the parents at the elementary school, and then most of the parents in the whole town. We had a local paper, the *Sandpiper Gazette*, that only printed every three weeks, but just my luck, they printed the week before the school board meeting, and the book challenge was the big headline:

MOTHER CHALLENGES HOMOSEXUAL BOOK IN LOCAL CLASSROOM

My friends really loved the phrase *homosexual book*, which made it sound like the book itself was gay and was going to start kissing the other gay books on the shelf.

Meanwhile the word in the headline that got to me the most was *Mother*. Because not only was the article front and center in the paper, but they'd interviewed my mom about what they called her "crusade."

"I don't think a teacher should determine what my child reads without my permission," she was quoted as saying. "My child should be raised on my agenda, not any teacher's. When my son grows up, he can read whatever he wants. But while he's still a child, it is up to his parents to protect him from the things he's not ready for."

It was humiliating.

I was too scared to tell my mother how humiliating it was. Plus, she was too busy on the phone, talking to other parents and other angry residents of Sandpiper Township, strategizing for the board meeting.

Allison's mom was also quoted in the article, saying, "This isn't the nineteenth century. The presence of gay people in our world is not something that should be hidden from children—it's something that should be celebrated. The whole point of education is to dispel ignorance and teach children about the world they live in. I don't know what world the other parents think our children live in, but it's not this world. If [the complaining parent] thinks that hiding books with gay content will prevent her son from knowing there are loving, wonderful gay people in our community and in our world, I have news for her: It's too late. He knows."

Allison's mom was right. I thought of Mr. Howe when I read this. And Curtis. And Kira's moms. If my mom really thought Rick and Oliver were the first gay people I'd ever known, she was so wrong. And Rick and Oliver weren't even real!

I wondered how my mom would respond to what Allison's mom was saying. But I guessed I had to wait until the school board meeting to find out.

The article said that Mr. Howe "declined to comment." When I went to school the next day, it was easy to see how exhausted he was. He was usually so energetic, but now he looked like he needed a long nap. He kept apologizing to the class for being so out of it.

Meanwhile, Allison didn't waste any time asking me if I'd gotten in touch with Bright. I could see other kids paying attention, and I could imagine them thinking that because I was my mother's son, there was no way I was on their side. I couldn't think of a way to tell them I hadn't used that Contact button, that I'd been too scared of being found out by my parents to do the one thing I'd promised to do.

So I lied.

"I sent him an email last night," I said. "He hasn't written back yet."

If I thought that would make it better, it only made it worse. At recess, everyone wanted me to check my email to see if Bright had responded. Allison even snuck me her phone after music class so I could use it to log in. I had to keep being surprised when I saw that there wasn't any reply.

If anyone in our class was on the anti-*Adventurers* side, they weren't saying it. Instead, all the kids were abuzz with ways to help Mr. Howe and the book at the board meeting we weren't supposed to go to without our parents. Most kids said their parents were okay with them reading the book—it was just that the ones who weren't, like my mom, were pretty loud about it. And it only took one parent to make a book challenge, not a majority.

"Maybe I'll kiss a boy at the meeting to show them we all know what gay means," Curtis suggested.

"Any boy in particular?" Patience asked. A couple of kids started to *ooooooh,* and Curtis blushed.

Luther looked at Curtis with something close to disgust.

"Dude," he said, "you don't want your first kiss to be at a *school board meeting.*"

"Not very romantic," Allison agreed.

"But it does make a point," Kira said. Then she added, "I'm sure I can ask my moms to kiss instead. It's kind of gross how often they do it in front of my friends. Not because they're lesbian. But because, like, who wants their parents to do that all the time?"

We all shook our heads. None of us did.

The conversation made me feel a little better as we headed back into class, because even if the adults were arguing across the front page of the local paper and across dozens of group chats, at least we kids knew what the right side was.

The a-little-better feeling collapsed, though, when I saw Mr. Howe again. The copies of *The Adventurers* were still stacked on the front table of the room, and I felt like they were Kryptonite to Mr. Howe, sapping him of all his superpowers.

He was suffering, and I couldn't even email an author.

When the final bell rang, kids raced out of class at the usual pace. I stayed behind. At first, I pretended to be looking for something in my desk. Then I pretended to be looking for something in my coat. Finally, Mr. Howe and I were the only ones left in the room.

He was at his desk, working on something. I wasn't even sure he knew I was there. I didn't want to disturb him, but at the same time I felt I couldn't leave the room without talking to him.

"Mr. Howe?" I said quietly.

He looked up and stopped writing. "What can I do for you, Donovan?"

I couldn't even look at him. I looked at the mug on his desk, the one with the big *B* on it.

"I'm sorry," I said.

He didn't say, "For what?" He knew for what. I looked up and saw he was even sadder now, facing me.

"Donovan," he said, "none of this is your fault. None of it. Do you understand?"

"But if I'd been reading the book, she wouldn't have been able to get it. Or if I'd kept it in my bag, she probably wouldn't have found it."

These were the facts I had to live with. The facts I couldn't tell anyone else.

"Donovan," Mr. Howe said again. At that moment a big, burly guy came through the open door, carrying a bookcase. I couldn't see the guy's face—it was blocked by the bookcase—but his voice was a happy growl.

"Bookcase delivery for the man I love!" he called out musically.

Mr. Howe stood up. "Do you need help? Be careful of your back!"

The big guy put the bookcase down in the empty corner to the right of the whiteboard, then laughed a big "WHEW!" through the room.

Mr. Howe shook his head, but he didn't seem nearly as sad anymore.

"Donovan," he said, "this is my husband, Bert. Bert, this is Donovan."

It's possible I made it up in my mind, but I thought I saw something click into place when Bert heard my name. Like he was translating the word *Donovan* into the phrase *the one whose mom started this whole mess.*

"It's lovely to meet you, Donovan," Bert said. Then he gestured to the front table. "Are these the books?"

"Yes," Mr. Howe said. "But you don't have to do that."

Bert waved him off. "You two finish up. I'll take care of the books."

Bert fiddled with the bookcase, then started to move the copies of *The Adventurers* there. As he did, Mr. Howe explained to me that he was tired of having the books just piled there, "as if they're evidence in a court case." It turned out that Bert made furniture for a living, and had this extra bookcase in his workshop, for the copies of *The Adventurers* and other books that were now in stacks around the room.

"I always joke his parents should have named him Know—so his name would be Know Howe," Mr. Howe said. He sat on the edge of his desk and gestured for me to sit on the desk in front of it.

"Look, Donovan," he continued, "I want to make sure you understand this. You are never responsible for your parents' actions. Never. Whatever they do, whatever they say, you cannot bear any of the blame for it."

"But I left the book out, and that's how she was able to read it," I said.

"I welcome her reading it," Mr. Howe said. "I never told you to hide it or any of the other books I've assigned in class. If she feels the way she does, this is a conversation we need to have. Do I wish it wasn't such a public conversation? Of course. But it's still an important conversation to have."

He looked over to where Bert was making sure all the spines were lined up on the shelves before he put on another stack.

"Look," Mr. Howe said, "I have to tell you, if this had come up in the nineties, when I was your age, I suspect my mom would have agreed with your mom. She wasn't ready to understand that I was gay, and when you're not ready to understand something, you become afraid of it. I figured things out pretty early, but it still took me years to tell my parents. And when I did, it took them even longer to adjust. It wasn't because they were homophobic; they just thought they knew me well, and this proved that they didn't know me quite as well as they'd thought. Eventually they understood—and I gave them some books to help them understand. Now, I'm not saying the same thing is happening here, in terms of who you are. But I think some of the parents who are most afraid of this book are actually afraid that the world you're growing up in isn't the world they grew up in. And rather than adjust, they think they can keep it the same. That never works, not in a free society."

Mr. Howe gestured to Bert. "See my husband there? There was a time when teachers didn't feel comfortable being out, letting the students know they were gay or had spouses or partners. And I'm sure in some parts of the country and other parts of the world, there's still the need to keep quiet. There's nothing wrong with keeping quiet if you feel you aren't safe. But I wasn't going to hide my life or my husband from you kids. How could I claim to be an educator while hiding such an essential truth from you? And you know what—while a couple of parents have been surprised over the years, or have had to open their minds a little more than they'd been planning to, most of the time, it's no big deal. And that's what Rick and Oliver's love should be, too. Whether or not you think they're gay, it's no big deal. It's not the point of the story. Being gay is not the point of my life or Bert's life. It's an important part of it, definitely. But it's not the point."

I thought I understood what he was saying, but I was also hung up on another question that was now stuck in my head. Something about the way Mr. Howe was talking to me made me feel I could say it out loud.

"Do you think my mom thinks I'm gay?" I asked.

Mr. Howe thought about his answer for a second, then said, "I don't know what she thinks, honestly. So all I can do is point out that whatever she thinks doesn't define you anyplace other than her mind. It's okay if you're gay. It's also okay if you're not gay. And it's okay if you haven't figured it out, because most of us don't figure it out when we're in fifth grade."

I didn't want to tell him I was pretty sure I liked girls, because I knew he was right—I didn't have to have it figured out.

Bert had now finished putting the books on the shelves. He kept moving them a little this way and a little that way, but I could tell it was only because he didn't want to interrupt our conversation.

"Is there anything else you want to talk about?" Mr. Howe asked. I sensed that he'd give me all the time I needed. But the truth was, there was another important thing I needed to do before the school closed for the day.

"No, I'm good," I told him. "Thank you."

"Anytime," Mr. Howe said. "Truly."

Bert stepped away from the shelf and said it was a pleasure to meet me.

"Great to meet you, too," I said. Even though Mr. Howe kept a photo of Bert on his desk, I thought that maybe I was the first student to meet him. This would be big news at recess.

As soon as I was out of class, I headed quickly to the

library. It was open an hour after school ended, so I knew it would be okay. But I also didn't know how long I would need to do what I had to do.

Ms. Guy was there at the front and smiled when I came in. Most of the computers were being used, but I found one near the back that was open. Before I could think too much about it, I went to Bright's website and double-checked the email address I'd memorized last night. Then I loaded up my email. This time, instead of checking for an email I knew wouldn't be there, I wrote a new one.

Dear Mr. Bright,

My name is Donovan and I am a fifth-grade student at D. Craig Walker Elementary School. I am writing to you because our teacher assigned us your book The Adventurers. Some parents, including my mother, made a book challenge against the book and there is going to be a school board meeting about it next week. I was hoping you could tell me whether Rick and Oliver in your book end up being boyfriends or if they are just friends because that's something we're trying to figure out. If you could write me back soon I would appreciate it because the meeting is next week.

Thank you,
Donovan Johnson

PS—I really loved the book. All of us did. My
copy was taken away but I got a library copy.
It was so good.

It almost took me a half hour just to type this one paragraph. It seemed weird to ask *Are Rick and Oliver gay?* And I also worried he would think I was like my mother and thought that was a bad thing. Even after I hit Send, I worried I hadn't said it right.

Amazingly, it only took a few seconds to get a response. Or at least it seemed amazing until I read the message.

Thank you for sending me a message. I am deep
into writing my new book right now and am
trying to avoid having email suck up all my
words. It may take me a few weeks to respond to
you—but I promise I will respond when I can.

Keep reading!
G. R. Bright

A few weeks?! We didn't have a few weeks.

I wanted to shake the computer . . . but didn't, because it was a library computer. So instead I stared at the screen, wondering what to do. Should I call his publisher and tell them it was an emergency? Or maybe see if our local bookstore could track him down using bookstore intelligence? Or was Bright off in a cabin somewhere, writing his new book, having no phone or internet, and therefore having no idea how much we needed him now?

Ms. Guy made an announcement that the library would be closing in five minutes. I sighed and went to shut my email. Right when my cursor was above the red dot to close the window, a new email appeared.

It was from Bright, and all it said was this:

Do you mean D. Craig Walker Elementary School in Sandpiper Township, Virginia?

six

Gideon and Roberto became a pair. Not a couple. (*Gideon would never have used that word.) Or boyfriends. (*Because, weirdly, girls were allowed to call their close friends who were girls *girlfriends,* but boys weren't allowed to call their close friends who were boys *boyfriends.*) They were a pair in the same way a pair of headphones was a pair—connected and sharing a music only they possessed.

As January started to turn its last corner, they found they were a pair surrounded by more and more couples. Because with Valentine's Day coming up, people wanted to be in a couple, even in fifth grade. First Darren started dating Cora. Then Jackson succumbed to April (*or maybe he just pretended to be succumbing, and really liked her). Then, much to Gideon's surprise, Joelle told him that she and Tucker were going out.

All Gideon could say to that was "Oh." Then, after Joelle had stared at him long enough, he added, "That's great!"

Gideon honestly wasn't sure it was great. They were his two best friends. It could be really messy if they broke up. Or maybe they'd leave him behind.

Seeing his expression, Joelle said, "Don't worry. We're still the three of us. And also, you have Roberto to hang out with. So it's not like we'll be leaving you *alone*."

Roberto had been sitting with them at the boy-girl lunch table for weeks now, and fit in as much as anybody who hadn't been going to Walker Elementary since kindergarten could. Gideon often found himself explaining what they were talking about—what had gone wrong on the third-grade field trip or what Mia's mom had done to the cupcakes she'd brought to class for Mia's birthday last year or why it was so hysterical that Jackson and April were a couple, considering April had punched him out in second grade.

Roberto didn't write these stories down in a notebook, but Gideon could see him taking them down in his memory (*even though he had no way of knowing how long they would stay there). It made everything a little more interesting, to have to explain it to someone else. Because in order to explain something, he had to find the story behind it. And Roberto made Gideon realize there were stories behind everything. (*Harriet the Spy could have told him that too, if she'd gone to their school.)

As Valentine's Day got closer, the pressure among the couples continued to build. It felt so old-fashioned to Gideon—the boys bragging about what they were going to do, and the girls bragging about what their boyfriends told them they were going to do. Usually something involving flowers. Or chocolate. Or a restaurant. Or all three. Gideon had never liked it when he'd been forced to give cards to every single person in his class . . . but he actually liked that much more than he liked everyone sectioning off into twos.

Roberto didn't seem to have any feelings about Valentine's Day that Gideon could notice. (*Gideon was paying close attention.) He didn't seem to be jumping into the fray of needing someone to buy chocolate for. Nor did he seem that worried that his February 14th might be valentine-free. The first time he even joined the valentine conversation was when Joelle brought it up at the lunch table, hinting to Tucker that homemade gifts were better than a bunch of flowers . . . as long as the homemade gift took a lot of hours to make.

"I could teach you how to knit her a scarf," Roberto offered.

"That's so sweet!" Joelle said. "You should totally do that!"

Tucker looked at Roberto with murder in his eyes. "Um . . . I can't. Because I've already planned . . . something else."

"Well, it better not be homemade cookies," Joelle said. "Because I know who makes the cookies at your house, and it isn't *you*."

Tucker sighed. Snagged.

"What are you guys doing for Valentine's Day?" Joelle asked Gideon and Roberto.

Does she mean each of us separately or does she mean us together? Gideon wondered.

Aloud this was shortened to him saying, "Together?"

Roberto looked at him strangely and said, "We haven't decided yet. But we'll do something. While all of you are on your *dates,* we'll be hanging out."

Gideon was surprised by this, but it also made sense. Couples went on dates. Pairs hung out. Therefore he and Roberto would hang out.

They'd been hanging out a lot, mostly at Roberto's house, where it wasn't against the rules to have a friend over after school. Roberto's mom was often there—even though Roberto's dad had gotten a great job, she hadn't been able to find one in their new town. Within a week of his first visit, she was treating Gideon like a member of their extended family.

Valentine's Day was a Friday that year. Roberto invited Gideon to sleep over. When Gideon asked his parents if that was okay, he was relieved to find they had made valentine plans of their own and were grateful that they didn't have to find a sitter.

That morning, Gideon came down to the kitchen for breakfast to find two heart-shaped boxes of chocolate on the table—a big one for him and a small one for Samson. (*On a previous Valentine's Day his mother had made the mistake of buying Gideon a chocolate turtle, which he'd refused to eat, because the idea of biting into a turtle was so deeply upsetting. He couldn't understand why his mother had put him in such a cruel situation.)

Normally, Gideon would have left his box of chocolates in the kitchen, and would have doled them out to himself one at a time, to such a prolonged degree that it might have been Easter by the time all the chocolates were gone. This time, though, he hoped his parents didn't notice when he took the box upstairs, so he could hide it in his backpack to take to school, and then to Roberto's.

Once he got to school, he was very aware that he was what seemed like the only person who wasn't parading his valentine in front of everyone else. Jackson made a big show of giving April a bracelet, telling her, "It's real gold." And then, when she didn't seem excited enough, he repeated it: "It's real gold."

The first thing Roberto asked Gideon when he got to class was what Tucker had ended up doing for Joelle. About five seconds later, Joelle came in wearing a red scarf, looking pleased. Tucker looked relieved.

As Ms. June started her lessons, Gideon pondered the word *valentine*.

On the one hand, it contained the word *evil*.

Valentine = An evil net

On the other hand, it contained the word *live*.

The whole day, Gideon kept the chocolates in his backpack. Even though he was hungry. Even though there were kids all around him eating their own chocolates. He didn't even say anything about them as he and Roberto walked over to Roberto's house. When they got there, he expected Roberto's mom to come out and greet them. Instead, Roberto explained that she'd driven into the city to pick up his dad so they could have what he called "a night out." Which left Gideon and Roberto to have a night in.

They got snacks from the kitchen, like they usually did, and then went into the den to play some Nintendo (*also like they usually did). Since it was Friday, homework didn't hover over their hours together. Something else hovered instead. Things felt so ordinary that Gideon kept the heart-box of chocolates in his bag. Roberto wasn't mentioning Valentine's Day at all. So maybe they weren't celebrating it. A pair, not a couple. Two friends hanging out on a February afternoon. Fourteen was just a number.

They played some *Super Mario Kart* and some *Final Fantasy V,* and even though this was something Gideon loved to do, especially on the couch next to Roberto, he wasn't as into it as he usually was. Valentine's Day wasn't only hovering—it was starting to retreat. And Gideon found that he didn't want it to, even if he wouldn't have been able to explain to himself why.

Finally, after a particularly strong run at *Mario Kart* on Roberto's part, Roberto paused the console and said, "I have something for you." He ran out of the room so quickly, Gideon didn't even have a chance to ask what. He could hear Roberto zipping around the house, and he felt slow in comparison.

When Roberto came back into the room, he had something behind his back, and enough mischief in his eyes that Gideon wouldn't have been surprised if it had been a Super Soaker. But instead it was an envelope, a red envelope.

"For you," Roberto said.

He didn't need to say it, because *GIDEON* was written in enthusiastic letters on the front of the envelope.

Gideon didn't have to ask Roberto if he should open it now—the answer was written across Roberto's face as enthusiastically as Gideon's name was written on the envelope.

Inside the envelope was a homemade card. It showed a turtle that looked a lot like Samson. The only difference was that all the spots on his shell were shaped like hearts.

Gideon opened the card. Inside it said:

Happy Valentine's Day
to
The Best Valentine in the Whole World

Love,
Roberto

Gideon felt his heart racing with happiness and beating with a nervous energy. He didn't know what to say, so he made a joke instead.

"Wow," he said. "The whole world. That's a lot."

Roberto sat back down next to him on the couch, turned so his knees were touching the side of Gideon's leg.

"Yes," Roberto said. "From the North Pole to the South Pole. From the bottom of the Grand Canyon to the top of the mountains in Yellowstone."

"I think you mean Yosemite," Gideon said. "Yellowstone doesn't have mountains. Yosemite has El Capitan."

"From the bottom of the Grand Canyon to the top of El Capitan, then!"

"But why?" Gideon asked. He couldn't help himself. "I haven't done anything!" Then, as soon as these words were out, he remembered the chocolates. "Wait!" he said, reaching for his backpack and taking out the heart-shaped box. "I did! I brought you this!"

He removed the plastic and sat back down on the couch, crisscross facing Roberto. Roberto shifted so he was sitting crisscross too, knees touching Gideon's. The box of chocolates sat in both of their laps.

Gideon removed the lid and then took out the piece of paper on top. He started to look at it, because it explained which fillings were in each piece of chocolate, but Roberto grabbed it away from him and threw it over his shoulder.

"That's cheating!" Roberto said. "Here."

He picked up a chocolate and broke it in half, revealing the coconut filling inside. He gave half to Gideon and kept half for himself. On the count of three, they put the halves in their mouths.

"Yum," Roberto said.

"Definitely," Gideon agreed.

Gideon chose the next piece. It was messier to split—a molten chocolate erupting onto his fingers. The two halves collapsed like demolished houses. Gideon was going to give up, but Roberto took one of the gooey chunks and popped it quickly into his mouth. Gideon did the same, then licked his fingers for good measure.

Roberto contemplated the next piece, then said, "I have an idea." He picked a rectangle of chocolate and held it up to Gideon. "I'll hold it in my teeth and you lean in and bite off your half."

He didn't wait for Gideon's answer. He placed the chocolate in his mouth, with a little more than half sticking out. Even while doing this, he managed to smile.

Gideon's heart raced even more. If he was the tortoise, his heart was the hare. And it was leaning him forward. It was letting him move through the space between them until there wasn't any space left. He put his lips around the chocolate, and he couldn't do that without also pressing his lips against Roberto's. Both of them bit down on the chocolate, and it split between them, filling their mouths with caramel sweetness. For a moment, they hung there, the tastes inseparable. Then they pulled back, a strand of the caramel stretching between them until it broke and fell onto Gideon's chin.

Roberto couldn't stop smiling. Gideon was shaking, but also he was okay.

"I love it," Roberto said.

And Gideon said, "Me too."

Now it was Gideon's turn. He picked up a large roundish chocolate.

"What do you think it is?" he asked.

"Maybe cherry," Roberto said. "Maybe hazelnut?"

Now it was Gideon's turn to smile.

"Let's see," he said.

He put half the chocolate in his mouth.

Roberto came to get the other half.

It tasted like roses, of all things.

They continued the game until there were only two chocolates left in the box. Most of their guesses were wrong. Most of their pass-offs lasted longer than they needed to. They ate so much chocolate that they didn't have any room for dinner. They ate so much chocolate that they crashed earlier than they'd planned, asleep before Roberto's parents came home. When Mr. and Mrs. Garcia did return, they peeked into Roberto's room and saw the two boys in Roberto's bed, still in their clothes, chocolate on their fingers and on their lips and on their shirts and pants, too.

Roberto's parents decided not to wake them, so it was in this way that Gideon and Roberto ended the happiest Valentine's Day they'd ever had.

Jumping to . . .

CHAPTER TWENTY-TWO:
NO TIME TO SPARE

"Where are they?" Rick asked, the edge in his voice so sharp it was surprising it didn't cut right through their command center.

The reinforcements they'd been promised hadn't arrived yet.

"McAllister is on the move," Melody reported, scanning the security footage she'd intercepted from Jacques Le Jacques's fortress. "We don't have any time left."

"We know what we have to do," Oliver said quietly, as if it was a truth he didn't want to admit.

Rick studied his friend, concerned. He hadn't been the same since they'd gotten onto Le Jacques's property. He acted like someone who, deep in his bones, knew he'd been here before.

Hesitation was a luxury they couldn't afford, so Rick made a snap judgment.

"Okay," he said. "We're going in." Oliver immediately reached for his pack, but Rick shook his head. "Not you and me. Me and Melody."

"What?" Oliver said. Rick had thought he'd look relieved, but instead he looked hurt.

"You stay here and hack the security system. Melody and I will go in and catch McAllister once and for all."

"I'm okay," Oliver argued. "I can do it."

"I've seen you look at those monitors," Rick said. "I've seen the way you shake when you see those gators."

Now Oliver was angry, exposed. "I told you, *I can do it.*"

Melody looked from Rick to Oliver, then back again. "*Guys,*" she said. "We don't have time for this. Oliver, if you say you can do it, I believe you. Rick, I understand why you're worried, but Oliver's never let you down, and he won't let you down now. Also, Oliver wouldn't know how to hack this security system even if I had days to train him. I need to get you in there, and I also need to be here to coordinate the reinforcements when they come. Now suit up and get out of here. If McAllister escapes on that helicopter and we're still stuck in this swamp, there will be no saying *see you later* to these alligators."

"Fine," Rick said, putting on his pack and checking his gear.

"I'm telling you, I'm okay," Oliver said, walking to the door and waiting for Rick there.

Rick tried to be convinced.

But he couldn't help noticing that Oliver, the possessor of the Doomsday Code, took a really deep breath before stepping outside.

7

I told everyone in my class that I'd heard from Bright, and that he'd asked for Mr. Howe's email address. He'd said he wanted to find out what he could do to help.

"But did he tell you if Rick and Oliver are gay?" Luther asked.

"It doesn't matter," Allison interrupted.

"That's right," I agreed. But the truth was, I hadn't felt comfortable asking the author that again. It felt personal. Maybe if we'd talked about the book a little bit more in our emails, I would have asked. But once I gave him Mr. Howe's contact info, it was like Bright was off to plot things with him, not me. There was no way Bright could know that my mom was the one who started everything, but still I knew that at some point he *would* know. And that had made me feel more shy.

I definitely was *not* going to tell my mom or dad that

I'd been in touch with the author of the book that was dividing my town. Actually, that wasn't fair—the book wasn't dividing anything. It was just a book. It was my mom who was doing the dividing, or at least a part of it. Preparing for the school board meeting had become a full-time job for her, with phone calls and meetings and late-night emails. After the initial accusations, nobody at school really mentioned my mom to me. And at the same time, my mom never acknowledged what any of my friends at school might have thought. It was like because she thought she'd prevented me from reading the book, she also thought I didn't know what was going on.

Mostly I tried to avoid her. And while my dad wouldn't have admitted to aiding this avoidance, when we were all forced to be in the same room together—usually over a meal—he took on most of the burden of conversation.

This worked fine until the night before the school board meeting. Dad had to work late, so Mom and I were home alone.

I hid away in my room and opened more textbooks than necessary, to create the illusion of an avalanche of homework. Still, I could hear her on the phone—*rallying the troops* was what she called it. And all I wanted to ask was *Why this war?*

I tried to block out the sound of her phone conversations by playing music louder than I usually did. This meant I also blocked out when she called me for dinner. I nearly jumped as high as the ceiling when she threw open the door and said, "That's too loud. It's time for dinner."

I felt about as excited as a prisoner would be when told he'd have the honor of dining with the warden. Even worse, the warden seemed to be in a good mood. She'd made mac and cheese, which was my favorite. (There was also broccoli, but I didn't mind the broccoli when there was mac and cheese because I could just drown it in the mac and cheese so it didn't taste like broccoli at all.)

Once we sat down, she asked me, "So how's school?"

This could only be a trick question. So I gave my usual answer.

"Fine."

If Dad had been there, this would have been his cue to start talking about something else, like the weather or football or the state of the economy. But without Dad there, there was instead . . . a follow-up question.

"Have the kids been giving you a hard time about our effort?"

She went there. She actually went there. And I was so surprised that I actually answered with the truth.

"They were giving me a hard time until I told them I was on their side. Now they don't give me a hard time at all."

For a second, nothing in the kitchen moved. The food sat there on our plates. The silverware stared at the ceiling, hoping the awkward moment would pass. The refrigerator hummed disapprovingly, *Not a good idea, Donovan.* And then some ice cubes decided to fall, crashing in the freezer as if they were calling out, *We've got to see THIS!*

The phone rang. I thought I was saved. But she didn't make any move to answer it.

"What do you mean?" she asked me.

I said, "I mean, I think it's a good book."

My mother speared a piece of broccoli. Put it in her mouth. Chewed. Made me wait. Swallowed.

The phone stopped ringing.

"Where did you get a copy of the book?" Mom asked. "Did Mr. Howe let you have one?"

I didn't want to get Ms. Guy in trouble, so I said, "I read Allison's copy. When she was done with it. Then I gave it back."

I ate some mac and cheese. It burned my tongue.

My mother didn't yell. She sighed.

Then she asked, "Why would you do that?" And before I could say anything, she answered, "No doubt because I told you not to." While I tried to think of another excuse, she went on. "I should have known that would happen. It's perfectly natural for you to be curious. But still, I wish you hadn't."

I actually felt bad for a second, because there were plenty of other things she'd wish I hadn't done, like getting in touch with the author. I wondered if there was any chance that would stay a secret.

She saw me thinking something, but had no idea what it was.

"There are so many books your teacher can choose from," she said. "So many great books. All I'm saying is that he should choose one of *those* books, not this one. I loved that you read *Johnny Tremain*. I still remember reading that when I was your age. And when you told me I had to read *A Long Walk to Water,* I was so glad you did, because that's a fantastic book. I'm not saying Mr. Howe makes bad choices or that he's a bad teacher. I think he's a very good teacher. He just chose the wrong book. And when parents think a teacher has chosen the wrong book, there's a process in place for us to say so. That's all that's happening here."

She made it sound so simple, so scientific, so commonsense. But it wasn't simple. Or scientific. Or commonsense.

Normally I would have kept my mouth shut.

Normally I would have kept my head down and eaten my dinner.

Normally I wouldn't have spoken because when a kid speaks in a way that is in opposition to an adult, adults call it *talking back.* And when they call it that, they never mean *talking back* is a good thing.

But I wasn't entirely myself at that moment. I wasn't normal. No, I felt something rise in me. It made my heart beat faster. It pumped my blood faster. It made my brain feel like it was coming into focus. It was something that was nameless to me, but it contained anger at unfairness, resistance to restriction, and an inability to remain silent even when I knew the easiest course would be silence. It was nameless as I felt it, but really it had a name: outrage.

I didn't yell.

I didn't knock my food off the table.

I didn't lock myself down, or shut myself up.

Instead, I started asking questions.

I began with: "Why do you think it's the wrong book?"

She'd been lifting a forkful of mac and cheese to her mouth. Now she held it there, as if for two seconds I'd stopped time.

"It's inappropriate," she said. Then she took a bite.

"Why do you think it's inappropriate?" I asked.

She swallowed.

"We aren't having this conversation, Donovan," she said.

"Why not?" I asked.

"You know why I think it's inappropriate."

"Not from you. Only from other kids who heard it from their parents. You didn't talk to me about it. Not once."

"I'm sorry if the other kids have been saying things—"

"No. It's not about that. This is about why you think a good book is a wrong book. I read it, Mom. Beginning to end. And I have no idea why you have a problem with it."

"It contains themes that aren't appropriate for kids your age."

"What themes?" I asked.

She sighed again. "This display of immaturity only proves my point, Donovan."

Okay, my outrage said. *It's time to use the words she won't use.*

"I don't know what world you think we live in, Mom," I said, remembering what Allison's mom had told the newspaper. "There are plenty of gay, lesbian, bi, trans, and nonbinary people on YouTube and TikTok and all the other things we watch. And other books I've read have had gay, lesbian, bi, trans, and nonbinary characters. Kira in our class has two moms, and there are other kids in our school with two moms or two dads or two parents who just want to be called parents. Some kids have nonbinary older siblings. And there's even a gay kid in my class."

"No, there isn't," Mom said.

"Yes, there is," I said. "How can you say 'No, there isn't'? That makes no sense."

"Nobody your age can know what he or she is. You're too young. You can decide those things later, but not now."

"But if that's true, isn't it also true that no one can know for sure that they're straight?"

I wasn't talking about myself. I was only trying to point out how weird her argument was. But the moment I said it, something new crossed her face. She looked helpless. It was the answer to a question I hadn't asked: *What are you afraid of?*

"We are who we are," I said. "And we'll be who we'll be. A book can make us *feel* that, but it can't *invent* that. It's already inside us."

"Donovan . . . what are you saying?"

I'm not coming out to you, I could have said. Because for all I felt at that moment, I wasn't gay. But at the same time I wanted her to understand what she was doing to all the kids who were or would be gay or lesbian or bi or trans or non-binary by trying to pull a book from our class just because it had one boy saying he loved another boy.

So what I told her was:

"I'm saying it's a good book and that Mr. Howe should teach it."

"Donovan, I'm on your side."

I thought of the Halloween costumes she'd sewn for me. The two of us sneaking off to an after-school movie and then telling Dad we'd been working. I remembered vacations where we climbed to the top of mountains. I remembered her reading me stories before I went to bed when I was little. I considered how much she knew I loved mac and cheese, and how that was the reason it was sitting in front of me right now.

"I know you're on my side," I told her. "Just not this one time. This one time you thought you were on my side, but you got it wrong."

My outrage was quieter now. What had risen a few minutes ago was now going away.

I ate some more. She ate some more. Whenever I looked at her, I could see her thinking something. I had no idea what it was.

Finally, I was done with all my mac and cheese and enough of my broccoli.

"Can I be excused?" I asked.

She nodded.

I pushed back my chair and carried my dishes to the sink. As I walked past the table to go back to my room, she said, "I love you, Donovan." And I said, "I love you, too."

We left it there.

seven

Roberto and Gideon didn't need to tell Roberto's mom what was happening between them, what they'd become for each other. She knew. And she let them know she knew without them having to tell her. She continued to welcome Gideon like family, and let him know he could come by whenever he wanted. When they got to Roberto's house after school, there'd usually be about ten minutes where they'd talk with her in the kitchen. Then, like a guardian angel who knew the best way to do her job, she stepped aside. She not only gave them space, but also made sure they knew it was entirely theirs. "I'm just going to go make some calls for an hour," she'd say. Or, "I'll be in the bedroom if you need me." Enough to let them know they wouldn't be disturbed, that their time together was something of value.

They didn't spend all their time kissing. There was also homework and *Super Mario Kart* and stupid shows on MTV. Roberto loved Madonna, and sometimes they'd blast her music and dance around the room, reenacting her moves in her videos (*"Material Girl" in particular) or making up some of their own (*"Burning Up" required some writhing on the ground, and sometimes water being thrown to "put the fire out"). Gideon couldn't imagine blasting music so loud without his parents intervening. But wherever Roberto and Gideon danced, they were safe.

This isn't to say they completely avoided Gideon's house. Gideon's parents paid much less attention to Roberto, but they were still happy to take the two boys to the movies on a Sunday afternoon or to let them have sleepovers as long as they promised not to stay up *too* late.

Every now and then, Roberto would also go home with Gideon after school, mostly when there was something Gideon needed from his house or if Gideon wasn't sure if he'd remembered to feed Samson in the morning.

One time, Roberto was playing with Samson on the floor of Gideon's bedroom when he said, quite randomly, "You know what? I think we should take Samson for a walk."

Gideon laughed, and Samson didn't offer any comment. Then Gideon, realizing he was up for some randomness, said, "Sure." He popped out of the bedroom for a second and then came back with a wheel of purple ribbon from his mom's gift-wrapping closet.

"We don't want him running away," Gideon said solemnly. Unlike with a dog, the ribbon couldn't really be tied around Samson's neck—he could easily pull his neck back into his shell and slip out of it. (*Gideon didn't want to tie it too tight.) So instead, Gideon tied the ribbon around Samson's shell. (*Samson didn't seem to mind.)

"Let's take him to the park," Roberto suggested.

"Would you like that?" Gideon asked Samson. Samson appeared to give a little nod.

About ten minutes later, they were in Leavitt Park, walking their turtle.

Samson, like most turtles, was not a fast walker. So Gideon and Roberto were the slowest pedestrians on the pedestrian path. Joggers would get really confused about why two boys were walking with such a deliberate lack of speed. Then they'd pass, turn back, and see the turtle leading the way. Almost all of them smiled. Some even stopped to make sure they were seeing what they were seeing. A few asked Gideon and Roberto what the turtle's name was. They were always happy to answer.

Gideon was holding the leash, but at one point, Roberto said, "Oh no! He's getting away!" and put his hand on top of Gideon's hand.

Roberto saw Gideon smile, and they walked like this for a while, totally in public. Roberto couldn't help but imagine Harriet M. Welsch sitting under a nearby tree, scribbling in her notebook about what she was seeing. They'd always be the Boys with the Turtle to her. She'd definitely think it was strange, but she wouldn't be able to stop writing about it.

Gideon loved seeing the joggers' faces, and other people's faces, as they passed. A mom was with her two little kids, and the kids thought Gideon, Roberto, and Samson were the funniest, most delightful thing they'd ever seen. They asked if they could pick the turtle up, and Gideon said yes. Their faces lit up as they held him.

Gently, they put Samson back down and their mom said thank you. Roberto took hold of Gideon's hand again, and they walked that way some more as the sun started to dip, all the green in the park glazed with gold.

I love this, Gideon thought.

I love Samson.

I love Roberto.

I love this park.

I love all of this.

He didn't need to rearrange any of the letters.

They were all in the right place.

Jumping to . . .

CHAPTER TWENTY-NINE:
GREATER THAN THE GATOR

Rick told himself it didn't matter whether Jacques Le Jacques was actually Oliver's father, as Jacques Le Jacques had claimed. Right now only two things mattered:

(1) Jacques Le Jacques was trapped in his own security chamber, under Melody's close watch.

(2) Rick was trapped too—in his case, by a hungry alligator that would soon be having him for lunch.

Even worse, McAllister—the mastermind of this whole evil situation—was about to make it safely to his backup escape vehicle, a souped-up motorcycle built for speed and evasion.

Only one thing stood in McAllister's way . . . and that one thing was named Oliver.

Rick saw his friend paralyzed by the choice he had to make: He could stop McAllister once and for all, or he could attempt to save Rick from a creature that had been giving Oliver nightmares for as long as he'd been able to dream.

He couldn't do both.

"Get him!" Rick shouted. "Stop McAllister! Go for the tires!"

The alligator didn't like this advice. It opened its mouth wide to show Rick all the teeth that were about to sink into his body. Then it moved forward.

Oliver, meanwhile, didn't move.

"Go!" Rick cried.

As if lit by a lightning strike, Oliver made his decision. He took a deep breath and lunged toward the alligator.

"AAAAAAACH!" Rick yelled, waving his arms. It was a ridiculous sound and it got the alligator's attention—which was exactly what Rick wanted.

Oliver, who was afraid of toy alligators—

Oliver, whose glasses now had cracks in both their lenses—

Oliver, who regularly lost in thumb-wrestling against both Melody and Rick—

Oliver, who never wanted to have anything to do with gators, was now jumping on the back of a gator.

He wanted to save Rick.

Both of them knew he only had one shot.

The good thing about people who are irrationally afraid of alligators is that they tend to spend an irrational amount of time online reading about how to wrestle alligators into submission, just in case.

Before the alligator could fully understand that there was a boy on its back, Oliver had thrown his jacket over its eyes with one hand and was using the other hand to press its neck to the ground with all his strength. At the same time, he was using his legs to prevent the gator from rolling. Pinned to the ground, the gator couldn't open its jaw.

Rick leapt forward to help his friend. As the gator retracted its eyes into its skull beneath the jacket and Oliver kept pinning it, Rick joined Oliver on its back, pressing against Oliver as he reached out for the soft skin under the gator's jaw. Then, as Oliver continued to use his weight to keep the gator's body down, Rick yanked the gator's jaw up ninety degrees, holding it close to his chest. Behind him, he could hear the gunning of the motorcycle's engine.

Even though the gator had now been wrestled into submission, Rick knew there was only so much time you could stay on top of an angry alligator.

"Ready for the dismount?" he asked Oliver.

"Yes!" Oliver said.

"Count of three."

On three, Oliver jumped off. On the count of four, Rick jammed the gator's head to the ground again, pinning it with his body. Then, gripping the gator by the neck, he threw it forward. It only skidded for about a foot, but that was enough for Rick to jump back and away.

Instead of turning to fight, the gator plunged back toward its tank. It would get its lunch elsewhere.

At the same time, Rick and Oliver saw the beautiful sight of Melody at the top of a staircase, flanked by other Adventurers. Even better, she held an industrial-size fishing rod.

With one fluid flick, she cast out a large hook—and landed it right on the collar of McAllister's leather jacket. Completely unprepared, he was imbalanced by her sudden tug.

The motorcycle made it out of the lair.

McAllister did not.

Rick and Oliver didn't hesitate. They jumped on McAllister just like they'd jumped on the gator. He cursed and flailed, but he couldn't get away. Mrs. Lindstrom, who always carried handcuffs for situations like this, appeared above Rick and Oliver and made McAllister's temporary capture a more permanent one.

Soon the Alligator Kingdom was crawling with police officers, federal officers, and other officers whose allegiance wasn't entirely clear to Rick.

"Looks like you got the catch of the day," Rick told Melody admiringly.

"Well, I wasn't the one who gave you the gator aid," she replied, tilting her head toward Oliver, who was silently staring down into the alligator tank.

Rick walked over to him and put a hand on his friend's shoulder. "You okay?" he asked.

"That was scary," Oliver said. "But . . ."

Rick waited for Oliver to finish his sentence. When he didn't, Rick said, "But . . . ?"

Oliver smiled, then put his hand on Rick's shoulder. "But I guess saving your life was worth it."

Rick smiled back. "Glad to hear it."

Oliver put his arm back to his side, and Rick did the same.

Rick sighed, watching the alligators still circling in the tank below them. "It's been quite a day, hasn't it?"

"Yup. But you know what—with everything that's happened, one thing's remained absolutely true."

"What?" Rick asked.

Now Oliver's smile was a full-on grin.

"I still hate Florida."

8

It felt like the whole town was planning to go to the school board meeting to argue about *The Adventurers*. Usually school board meetings happened in a small room in Town Hall. But because of the expected attendance, this meeting was going to be held in the high school auditorium.

Even though kids weren't specifically invited to school board meetings, there wasn't a rule that said they couldn't come. So most of Mr. Howe's class was planning to go—especially because Mr. Howe let slip that G. R. Bright himself was going to attend.

Still, even if kids were allowed to go, they needed their parents for transportation. Or at least I did.

It had been a tense twenty-four hours in our house. My mother hadn't said anything more to me about the book or the challenge, but she must have said something to my father when he'd gotten home, because in the morning, Dad seemed to be working extra hard to be on all sides of any conversation.

The school board meeting was at six. I went home immediately after school, then waited in my room for the right time to raise the subject of me going. I knew Mom would want to get there early, so I wasn't surprised when Dad was home at five. I went downstairs right after.

I'd put on a shirt and tie. I wanted them to know I was serious.

Dad was still in his suit from work. He was looking at a magazine in the kitchen when I came in. Mom was in her room, getting ready.

"You look nice," Dad said when he saw me.

"Thanks," I replied. "I'm dressed up because . . . well . . . because I need to go to the meeting with you. All the other kids from our class will be there. I have to be there too. They won't understand if I'm not."

Dad put down the magazine.

"Okay," he said. "Let me go discuss this with your mother. We should be heading out in about ten minutes."

He left the room and I stayed quiet, trying to overhear their conversation. But there must not have been any shouting, because I couldn't hear a thing.

A few minutes later, Dad came back into the kitchen.

"All set," he told me. "Wanna split a PB&J with me? I have no idea how long this thing's going to be."

"How about we each have our own?"

"You have yourself a deal."

Dad got to work putting the sandwiches together—one for me, one for him, and one for Mom. She came in right as he was finishing.

"How do I look?" she asked.

"Great," Dad said.

"You look nice," I said.

It was true. She was wearing her favorite maroon suit.

She also looked really nervous.

The phone rang and Mom answered, giving the person directions to the high school.

"Yes, yes . . . I really appreciate that," Mom said at the end of the call. "Either way, it'll be nice to have a decision."

After we finished our sandwiches, Mom took a deep breath, exhaled, and said, "Let's go."

We didn't talk about what was happening as we drove over. I didn't tell her I thought she was wrong, and she didn't tell me she thought I was wrong. We just listened to the news on the radio.

We weren't the first people at the high school, but we were definitely there before most other people. Some parents came over as soon as we got there and started to circle my mom, asking her questions or making statements about how sure they were that they'd win. Dad said he would go get us seats. As I followed him inside the auditorium, I saw Mr. Howe and Bert along with a few kids from our class and their parents, all sitting in one area. Immediately I knew that was where I needed to be.

"Dad," I said, "I'm going over there with my friends, okay?"

My father looked stumped. Then, after a moment's thought, he said, "All right. But I'll keep a seat here—just in case you change your mind."

"Thanks, Dad," I said. He gave me a little smile, then got some seats near one of the microphones they'd put in the aisles for people to use when they spoke to the board.

I shuffled through a row of seats to get to Mr. Howe and my class. Allison saw me coming over and called out my name, as if my appearance deserved to be announced. She even gave me a hug when I showed up, and so did her mom. I could see one or two other kids explain to their parents who I was, but I tried to ignore that.

"Awesome to see you here," Mr. Howe said. "And awesome that you could join us."

He explained to a bunch of the class how the hearing would work. The side filing the complaint (the complainers?) would speak first. Then the side defending the book would speak. Each side would have an hour. Then the review committee would give their recommendation. After taking this into consideration, the school board would vote on whether the book could remain in Mr. Howe's class or not.

As Mr. Howe explained this, more and more people entered the room to take their seats. Out of the corner of my eye, I saw my mother come in and find my father. Then I saw her ask a question. She looked my way after he answered, then turned back to the front of the room, where the school board members were taking their places at a table set up with ten chairs.

Once Mr. Howe was done explaining the hearing to us, he looked to the door and his face lit up.

"You made it!" he called out.

"I did!" a voice called back.

Mr. Howe stepped into the aisle and immediately was caught in a big, long hug by a man in a blue suit. They laughed, took a look at each other, then hugged again. When Mr. Howe introduced the man to Bert, Bert hugged him too.

"Kids," Mr. Howe said, "this is G. R. Bright. An old friend, and the author of *The Adventurers*."

A few of the kids gasped. I started to sweat, the sudden nervousness pouring out of me. This was the man I'd written to. This was the man who'd invented Rick and Oliver. I couldn't believe it.

"Which one of you is Donovan?" Bright asked.

Mr. Howe smiled and gestured to me. "Right here."

Bright held out his hand and I shook it.

"It's an honor," I told him.

"The honor's all mine, I assure you."

"He's not here to speak," Mr. Howe told us. "We're not going to tell anyone else he's here. He's just here to support us as we support his book. Do you understand?"

We all said we understood. Even the parents.

"Great!" Mr. Howe said. "Now I want to make some more introductions."

Soon Bright was shaking hands with Allison and her parents, and Kira and her parents, and Curtis and his parents, and anyone else he could reach. A few kids had their personal copies of *The Adventurers* with them, but Mr. Howe asked them to wait to get them signed, since people seeing him sign the books would know who he was.

"If all goes well, he'll drop by our class tomorrow," Mr. Howe promised. Then he and Bright started talking some more with Kira and her moms.

"Why doesn't he want to say something?" I asked Bert.

"Because the book's on trial here, not him," Bert replied. "I'll bet when he was a high school student here, he never would've imagined that he'd be back in this auditorium with half the town talking about a book he'd written."

"He went here?!" I said. "To *this school*?"

Bert smiled. "He even went to Walker Elementary."

Now it all made sense.

"Is that why Mr. Howe picked the book?" I asked Bert.

"No," Bert said. "He picked it because he liked it and thought the class would like it. But it's definitely the reason he read it in the first place."

The auditorium was filling up and getting pretty loud. I dared another look at my parents and saw that they weren't talking with anyone else, just sitting in their seats, talking to each other. The seat my dad had saved remained empty next to them.

"This school board meeting will soon be in session—

please take your seats," someone on the stage announced. When people kept chatting, the announcement was repeated with a little less politeness and a little more force. People got the message and started to sit down, their voices kept low.

"Here we go," Bright said to Mr. Howe.

Mr. Howe sighed worriedly. "Yes, here we go."

Bright sat down on one side of Mr. Howe, Bert on the other. I was right behind Bright, next to Allison.

The meeting began. There was some business to attend to that I didn't really understand, and then the school board president brought up the book challenge and explained the procedure in much the same way Mr. Howe had explained it to us.

The school board president said that anyone with concerns about *The Adventurers* could now approach the microphones in either aisle. She explained that in order to get to as many people as possible, comments would be limited to two minutes per speaker.

I looked over to where my parents were sitting. I expected the audience to part like a sea in order to let my mom speak first. I saw lots of parents in her section looking her way.

But she didn't stand up.

She didn't move.

My father leaned over and whispered something to her.

She shook her head.

Other people stepped up to the microphone.

Maybe she wants to go last, I thought.

Another parent from our class, Tarah's mom, kicked things off. She said a lot of what my mom had said to me at dinner—that Mr. Howe was a great teacher who usually taught "appropriate" books, but this time he'd made "an error of judgment" and had chosen a book that "the students aren't ready for." She said she understood that students "in a high school setting" could be "exposed" to "different identities" but that in elementary school and middle school it was "the parents' job" to make sure that "thoughts aren't put in kids' heads that they can't handle yet."

When she was done, there was applause. Both my mom and dad were clapping.

Amelia's parents spoke next. They actually felt comfortable saying the word *gay,* if only in the context of "We have nothing against gay people or adults who live the gay lifestyle," but they didn't want their own daughter "indoctrinated" by "assigned reading material."

More applause.

Bert whispered, "A synonym for 'live the gay lifestyle' is . . ."

". . . *gay,*" one of Kira's moms whispered back. "If only these people who *live the straight lifestyle* could understand that."

Three more parents spoke, saying basically the same things others had said. The third one, though, added, "And for another thing—it's not even a good book. It's just a silly adventure story. It's not a work of art we're talking about."

"Oof!" Bright said quietly. Then he and Mr. Howe laughed.

I kept looking at my mom, waiting for her to stand and take her place at the microphone. Instead she kept applauding, and smiling at people when their statements were finished.

Things began to go wrong with the next speaker. He was old and cranky, and he started his comments with "Homosexuality is a sin. It is an evil abomination. And it is the role of our schools to smite it out before it occurs."

"Oh boy," Bert said. "Fast-forward to the smiting."

The school board president tried to interrupt, saying this was a discussion about a specific book, and audience comments should be limited to the book and its merits.

The speaker basically ignored her. "Any teacher who teaches homosexuality should be put on the first train out of town," he said. Then he brought up other things not worth repeating here, blaming homosexuality for everything short of bad weather.

"I'm sorry, your time is up," the school board president said decisively. When the man tried to keep talking, his microphone was cut off.

Some people applauded. I couldn't tell whether it was for the man or for the microphone being cut off.

Unfortunately, the woman behind him had similar ideas. Not quite as into the conspiracy theories, but she made it clear that she felt being gay was wrong, and anything that might show kids it was okay to be gay was also therefore wrong. She even said, "I don't need to read this book to know it's evil." Because she was polite and not ranting like the guy before her, she got a little more applause at the end.

My parents, I noticed, were not clapping.

"I can't believe this," someone behind me said. I looked and saw it was Curtis.

"This is so stupid," Allison agreed, turning around and reaching out her hand to put it consolingly on Curtis's leg. "They're not talking about you, because they don't know you. You can't listen to insults from people who've never met you." A few people around us chimed in to agree.

Meanwhile, a parent of a high school student had gotten the mic and said that she would like to "disavow" the previous two speakers, and would like to reiterate that the book challenge wasn't an antigay challenge, but was about when it was "appropriate" to "teach kids about homosexuality."

This made no sense to me. It was like saying the only way we would have known that gay people existed was by reading about it in *The Adventurers*. Or that gay people themselves wouldn't know who they were until they were "taught" about it.

The next speaker might not have read the whole book, but he'd certainly read the ending. With utter disgust, he recited, " 'At that moment Rick knew just how *deeply* he *loved* Oliver, and Oliver knew just how *deeply* he *loved* Rick,' " saying *loved* as if it really meant something dirty. Then he started to talk about "innocent children" being "seduced" into a "life of sin."

I could see how tense this made Bright—it was clear he wanted to jump to his feet and object.

But instead other people objected for him. A huge round of boos started to come from the audience, mostly from kids who looked like high school students.

This only made the speaker angrier. "It's not okay to be gay!" he yelled to the students.

And in response, they started to chant . . .

It's okay to be gay.

It's okay to be gay.

It's okay to be gay.

We all started chiming in. Even though it wasn't the whole auditorium, it felt loud enough to be the whole auditorium.

The school board president let it go on for about half a minute, then called for order. Only she didn't go "Order! Order!" Instead she said, "We hear you. But we need to let the people challenging the book finish their allotted time."

I looked at my watch—there were only ten minutes left for their side. I assumed my mom would stand up now, that she would take her place to wrap it up.

I wasn't the only person. Tarah's mom was leaning over Mom's shoulder, talking to her.

But, again, Mom shook her head. I had no idea what was going on. It wasn't like my mom to be shy. But it also wasn't like my mom to say something she didn't believe. Did this mean she was changing her mind? Had something I'd said at dinner gotten through to her?

Or did she simply think that everything that needed to be said had already been said by other people?

The mom of a third grader spoke last. She said she'd been on the committee of parents who'd supported the challenge. She told the board, "There have been people who've spoken this evening who have said things we find baseless and abhorrent, and we want to be clear that we are not advocating anything other than the removal of this one book from the fifth-grade curriculum." Which was easy for her to say; I couldn't help but feel that the challenge had opened the door and the sin-talkers had walked right through it.

I half expected the school board president to ask, "Where's the parent who filed the complaint? Why hasn't she spoken?" But that's not what happened. Instead, she said it was time for the people who wanted to defend the book to speak.

There was a rush to the microphones. Mr. Howe didn't get to the aisle nearly as quickly as the high school students. But someone must have explained who he was, because they all stepped aside so he could go first.

After introducing himself as the teacher who'd chosen *The Adventurers* for his class, Mr. Howe got right to the point.

"The nature of Rick and Oliver's love is completely open to interpretation. But for the sake of this forum, let us assume that they are, in fact, gay. What, then, are the grounds for complaint? We are told that having a book with two gay characters is 'inappropriate'—but what does that really mean? And, just as important, what does that say to our students? I will tell you: It says that being gay is inappropriate. It says that it is shameful. It says that it is something you become instead of something that you are. It sends the message that if you don't read about it, it will go away. It sends the message that it *should* go away.

"Well. Let me be the first to say it tonight: There is nothing 'inappropriate' about being gay or lesbian or bisexual or transgender or nonbinary or questioning or any other identity within the LGBTQIA+ spectrum. There is nothing sinful about it. There is nothing to be ashamed of. There is nothing about being queer that deserves censorship rather than expression. Nothing. This should not be a matter of debate, because a person's humanity should never be a matter of debate. Instead, it is a matter of the highest principle we can aspire to, which is equality.

"I know that if you've spent your lives being told an identity is wrong, or sinful, or inappropriate, it's hard to wrap your mind around the fact that everything you've been told is bigotry. I grew up in this town. I know my parents loved me very much. But I also know that if this meeting had happened when I was a kid, my parents would have been among the people challenging this book. They would have done it out of fear. Not of the book, but of who I was then and who I was going to grow up to be. They would have been desperate to control it, to force my world into the shape they were told it was supposed to be. But they would have been wrong to do so, and ultimately they would have failed. Because even if they'd been able to control every single book I'd read as a child, I still would have grown up to be the gay, married, proud teacher who stands before you. In challenging a book, they would have been trying to turn off a tap, when who I am is actually an ocean.

"I'm happy to see there are many younger and no doubt wiser people behind me waiting to speak. I am eager to give them the floor. But I want to end by saying this: I hope to keep teaching *The Adventurers* in my class, as well as other books with LGBTQIA+ characters. I hope you will do the right thing and allow me to do so. But even if you pull all the queer books from our class, even if you could manage to somehow pull all the queer books from this town, I guarantee you, you will not stop us from being who we are. The worst damage you can do is to make the more vulnerable of us feel bad about it. But you cannot hold back the ocean. The ocean will not be contained in such a way."

As soon as he was done, we all started clapping and cheering, and our section was so loud, it was hard to tell at first that so many other people in the audience were clapping and cheering too. People were standing, whooping. Even some of the members of the school board were standing and clapping. Mr. Howe came back to us and Bert gave him the biggest hug and kiss, and then Bright gave him the second-biggest hug, and I think if there hadn't been seats in the way, our whole class would have given him the biggest group hug in town history.

The students started chanting again:

It's okay to be gay.

It's okay to be gay.

Finally, the auditorium quieted enough so the next speaker could begin. They said they were a nonbinary student at the high school, and wanted to share with the board what the books they had read as a kid meant to them. "These books didn't make me who I am," they said. "But they showed me I wasn't alone, long before I met other kids like me. How dare you try to take away that belonging and security from other kids."

More teenagers and adults told their stories. Allison's parents and other parents talked about the conversations *The Adventurers* had allowed them to have with their children, whether they were LGBTQIA+ or not.

The line to speak was getting longer and longer. Then, as they did for Mr. Howe, people stepped aside to let someone go to the front. It wasn't until he got there that I realized it was Curtis.

As soon as he got near the mic, his parents jumped up and rushed into the aisle. I thought they were going to try to stop him, because saying you're gay to your friends and saying you're gay to the whole town are two very different things. But when he stepped up to the mic, they didn't block him or pull him away. No, they stood behind him. His dad put a hand on his back for a second, just to let him know they were there.

"Hello," Curtis said softly. I could see a few people on the stage lean forward to hear him. "My name is Curtis. Mr. Howe is my teacher. I want to tell everyone here that I am gay. I think it's important you know that. A lot of the people here have been talking like there aren't any gay kids in Mr. Howe's class. They say that kids like me aren't ready to read about Rick and Oliver. But they have that wrong. There are plenty of fifth graders who are LGBTQIA+. Some of us are ready to talk about it. Some of us want to keep it to ourselves. Some of us still need to figure it out. Being ready is our choice, not yours. My parents say that telling someone who you really are is a gift you give to them, not something you owe them. My parents are right. You cannot completely ignore us. You cannot say there can't be books about kids like us. You can't say you're protecting us when you're trying to stop us from being ourselves. I just want to tell you that I loved *The Adventurers* and I love Mr. Howe's class. I think if you want to know what kids really need, then you should talk to us. So now I'm telling you what we need: more books, not fewer books. More love, not less love. Thank you."

This time, nobody hesitated to get to their feet. As Curtis turned to his parents and they hugged him, the auditorium rocked with cheers and applause. I looked over and even my parents were standing and clapping. My voice was going hoarse from yelling so loud. When Curtis got back to us, there was so much hugging and high-fiving. A few of the adults were crying, too. When Curtis finally sat down in his seat, he looked exhausted . . . but also like the exhaustion was totally worth it.

There was time for a few more speakers. When an old man got up to the microphone, I thought for a second that maybe someone from the other side had infiltrated our side. But instead of starting by saying that "homosexuality is a sin," he introduced himself and said that he and his husband had been together for over forty years.

"Just like Rick and Oliver, we have had many adventures and been to many places," he told us. "We haven't wrestled any alligators or escaped from any cages, but we have had to wrestle against a world that has told us our love doesn't count and we have had to escape through the bars of other people's prejudices. Especially after all the inspiring stories from so many people two generations below mine, I just wanted to say the story of love and happiness isn't only to be found in novels. It's our true story, and it's one that I've lived for most of my life. I hope this school board will see the sense of that, and will reject the nonsense of this book challenge."

After he was done, the school board president said, "I would like to thank all the speakers we've just heard from. Now I would like to ask Principal Woodson for her committee's recommendation."

Principal Woodson walked up to one of the microphones and said, "Thank you, Ms. Scoppettone. Our committee, made up of administrators, parents, our school librarian, and two teachers from other schools in our system, has now read and discussed *The Adventurers,* taking into consideration its literary merit, its themes, the concerns of the challenge that was filed, and Mr. Howe's reasons for teaching the book within his class. It is our unanimous recommendation that the school board reject the challenge and allow the book to continue to be taught in Mr. Howe's class."

All the students and parents around me cheered as if someone had just hit a home run. Bright put his hand on Mr. Howe's shoulder and squeezed. Bert wiped away some tears.

"Thank you, Principal Woodson," the school board president said. "With this recommendation and the comments made this evening in mind, the school board will now take its vote. Secretary Jenkins, will you call the roll? An *aye* will uphold the teacher's use of the text; a *nay* will be a vote for the book's removal from the classroom."

"Anderson?"

"*Aye.*"

"Block?"

"*Aye.*"

"Boonton?"

"*Nay.*"

Allison took my hand and squeezed. I closed my eyes and kept count.

"Aye."

"Nay."

"Aye."

"Aye."

"Aye."

On that sixth *aye,* the crowd erupted. There were ten people on the board, so even if the last two votes were *nay,* we had won.

The school board president called for order, but there was no getting order back. Allison's parents hugged her. Curtis's parents hugged him.

My parents were on the other side of the room.

"Hey," I heard someone say. It was G. R. Bright, turning back to look at me. "Good work." Then Allison stopped hugging her parents and started hugging me. The last votes (one *aye* and one *nay*) were tallied, and then the school board president adjourned the meeting.

There was more cheering and a lot of beaming smiles.

I tuned back in and Bright and Mr. Howe were talking in front of me.

"Are you sure you don't want to stay?" Mr. Howe asked. "It wouldn't hurt to let everyone know you were here."

"Nah," Bright said. "I'll drop by your class tomorrow."

Mr. Howe's face lit up. "I'd love that."

They hugged again.

"Thank you, Gideon," Bright said.

"Thank *you,* Roberto," Mr. Howe replied.

People were already crowding around to congratulate Mr. Howe. I watched as the author of *The Adventurers* walked down the aisle and out the door. When he lifted his legs, I could see he was wearing a pair of purple socks.

Someone's parent pointed out it was a school night, and suddenly everyone was being bundled back into their coats, readying to go. My parents had already left their seats; I assumed they would be waiting for me in the lobby.

I said goodbye to Allison and Curtis and Kira and Mr. Howe and Bert. I knew I was making my parents wait, and probably shouldn't. When I walked into the lobby, I saw a few people consoling my mom, but she just waved it off, thanked people for trying. When she saw me coming, she told them she had to leave. She and Dad walked over to me before I could walk over to them.

"Let's go," Dad said.

We headed quickly to the car. Mom thanked a few more people as we passed them, but she didn't stay to talk.

Once we got into the car, it was really quiet. I still had questions. Why hadn't my mom spoken? Why had she been a part of Curtis's standing ovation? But the questions weren't fueled by any outrage, just curiosity. And my curiosity could wait for now.

Finally, after we were out of the high school parking lot and halfway home, Dad spoke up.

"It's over now," he said. "All over."

"Yes," Mom said. "It is."

"*Amen*," I added. And something about the relief in my voice made both of my parents laugh.

"Who's hungry?" Dad asked.

"Me!" Mom and I both chimed.

Dad smiled. "Okay . . . where should we go?"

As I leaned back in my seat and let them figure out where we'd have dinner, I wished this whole story had been a book that had been handed to my mom, and that she'd been able to read the final pages first. Maybe then, things would have been different. Maybe then, she would have understood enough to change what she did.

Later that night, when she came in to say good night, my mother would thank me . . . not so much for opening her eyes, but for turning her head a little so she could focus on the right thing. She'd tell me that at first she had been convinced that my classmates and I weren't ready to read about two boys in love. But ultimately she realized that, no, she wasn't thinking about me and my friends. She was thinking about her and her friends, when they'd been in fifth grade. And the world had changed a lot since then. For the better. What I'd said at the dinner table had turned her head to see that. And what she'd seen at the school board meeting had made it clearer.

I would be happy to hear that. But for now, I was happy that we weren't talking about it anymore, and that we were heading to dinner as a family. I gazed out the window until I heard my mom say, "Here."

I looked up and saw she was handing me a copy of *The Adventurers*. She must have had it in her bag the whole time.

"Thank you," I said, putting it in my lap. My father turned off the news and started to whistle along to some music.

I smiled and began to reread the book from the beginning. I was looking forward to talking about it in class the next day.

And after that . . . I wondered what Mr. Howe would assign us next.

Jumping to . . .

fourteen

No matter how much Roberto protested and pouted and complained and lobbied, there wasn't anything he could do to change the simple fact:

His family was moving back to Miami.

It was heartbreaking for his mom. She knew how much Gideon meant to Roberto. But she was also so happy to be returning to their family, to the city she felt they never should have left.

"You can call him," she assured Roberto. "You can write letters. We'll even get AOL so you can get one of those email addresses and write to him that way."

Roberto had told Gideon as soon as he'd found out the news, so for the rest of the school year, they'd existed with the cloud of Roberto's departure over their heads. Joelle and Tucker could see the cloud, and they tried to break through it sometimes, asking Roberto and Gideon to go on double dates even though nobody called them double dates. Joelle and Tucker also understood when Gideon spent all his time with Roberto, and knew that once Roberto was gone, they'd have to step into the space Roberto would leave behind before it became large enough for Gideon to lose himself in.

On the last night, Gideon slept over at Roberto's house. Most of Roberto's room was packed up, but the bed was still made, and the blankets were still welcoming. They talked and kissed for as long as they could stay awake, then Gideon fell asleep with his head on Roberto's chest.

Roberto stayed awake most of the rest of the night, just so he could stare at the ceiling and feel the closeness of Gideon's breathing and the gentle sounds of his breath.

The movers came early in the morning, and Gideon knew it was time for him to leave. He couldn't believe it was happening, but he also knew he couldn't deny it was happening. They'd sworn to keep in touch, and he knew they would. But first there would be this big, temporary goodbye.

Roberto's mom came to the door of Roberto's room and told them they had about ten more minutes.

"Okay," Roberto said. Then he opened an otherwise empty desk drawer and took out a box.

"I got you something," he said.

Gideon smiled. "I got you something too."

Their boxes were the exact same size.

Roberto's box for Gideon contained what at first looked like a crystal turtle with a multicolored shell. But when Gideon looked closer, he saw what it really was: The shell acted as a kaleidoscope, refracting an image into bright fragments of color. When Gideon lifted the shell, he saw that underneath was a photo of Roberto leaning his head on Gideon's shoulder as they watched a movie together. Roberto's mother must have taken it when neither of them had been looking. It was such a sweet photo, and when Gideon closed the shell again, he saw how the turtle captured some of the music of the moment, taking the image and breaking it into something like feeling. The brightness of their togetherness, reflected in a shell.

"I love it," Gideon said. "Now open yours."

Inside Roberto's box was a silver turtle, so much like Samson that Roberto could believe that Samson had posed for it. The only difference was the silver, and the fact that when he turned it over, there was an inscription.

Roberto H. Garcia
Great
Rare
Bright

"I love it," Roberto said. "I'll keep it with me always."

And he would.

Roberto's lips touched Gideon's lips.

Gideon's tears touched Roberto's tears.

Roberto's arms wrapped around Gideon's body.

Gideon's arms wrapped around Roberto's body.

Time stopped long enough to deepen into a memory, and then time moved quickly again.

"Write something about me someday," Gideon said.

Roberto smiled and said, "I just might." (*He did.)

For an adult, six months is nothing. You can go six months without seeing your best friend. You can stay in the same spot and do the same thing for six months and not even notice. It's just a short stretch in a long life, and unless you're in love or in the midst of a big change, you barely even notice it until one day six months are gone.

But when you're a kid, six months can mean everything. A boy can walk into your class that first day and he can change your life entirely by the time he leaves six months later. And if you're the boy walking into that class, the same thing can happen. You can't imagine who you were before he showed you who you were meant to be.

Neither Roberto nor Gideon will actually use the word *goodbye*. To use it, they feel, would be to call it into being.

And in that farewell moment, it won't occur to either of them to say thank you, even though what they feel as much as love is gratitude. The thank you will come later, as the memory rises again. They will see what they were to each other, and they will be grateful, time after time after time.

"Good luck on your adventure," Gideon whispers to Roberto.

"You too," Roberto whispers back.

One more kiss.

One more hug.

They will never leave one another's lives.

Jumping to . . .

CHAPTER THIRTY-FOUR:
THE END . . .
AND THE BEGINNING

The trailer seemed strange without Melody around. Rick understood why she'd moved on—defeating McAllister wouldn't do a lick of good if his second-in-command, the Snake Goddess, wasn't captured too. The thing Rick didn't really understand was why he hadn't gone with her.

He didn't like the idea of adventures going on without him. But he also didn't like the idea of leaving right now.

Oliver's alligator nightmares hadn't gone away. If anything, they now felt more real, more detailed. Rick could hear him crying out as he woke up. If Rick asked what was wrong, Oliver would try to downplay it, saying it was just leftover nerves from what had gone down in Florida. He said it would go away over time. Rick wasn't so sure.

Rick wasn't awake now because of Oliver making noise, but because of a silence so absolute there was no way Oliver was around. With the threat of attack temporarily lessened, they'd moved the trailer aboveground, so a muted light was coming through the windows.

Rick threw on a bathrobe and walked outside. It was dawn, the grass wet with dew, the sky on the verge of color. Oliver, also wrapped in a bathrobe, hadn't walked too far away. He stood at the edge of the hill, looking at the spot where the sun would soon rise.

Oliver didn't seem surprised when Rick came up to him.

"You're up early," Rick said.

"My thoughts woke me up," Oliver explained. Then, referencing the now-imprisoned Jacques Le Jacques, he said, "It's really weird to finally find out you have family and realize you don't want to have anything to do with them."

"He's not your family," Rick assured Oliver. "You get to decide."

Oliver nodded, and as he angled his head down, the sun tilted its head above the horizon.

"That's pretty," Rick observed.

Oliver thought it was pretty too, but he had more important things on his mind. He needed to get them *off* his mind, and Rick was the only person he wanted to give them to.

He turned and looked at his friend for a second, the way the sun cast its glow across his welcoming, delighted face.

"Look," Oliver said, "I love it here. And I know what we do, fighting evil, is important. But how would you feel if we . . . went to school. Like, a regular school. Just to be around other kids and to do things like go to movies and complain about homework and have friends who don't always have to save our lives. How would you feel about that?"

Rick turned away from the sunrise and turned toward his friend. He took in the question and thought about it a second. Then he smiled.

"You know I'm always up for a challenge," he replied. "Wherever you want to go, whatever you want to do, count me in."

Now Oliver smiled back, all his nervousness gone. They watched each other and they watched the sunrise, and the way they felt, it was just about the same thing.

At that moment Rick knew just how deeply he loved Oliver, and Oliver knew just how deeply he loved Rick, and the understanding of this moment would lead them to much of the happiness and adventure that came next.

THE END

AUTHOR'S NOTE

There are many books that have led up to this book—not just books I've written myself, but books that came before mine that made my books possible. I would like to acknowledge many of them here.

The first openly queer book by an openly queer author for kids or teens that I knew about was Nancy Garden's *Annie on My Mind*. I was lucky to meet her and hang out with her early in my career, and am grateful that I got to thank her and, hopefully, prove myself worthy of the path she created. This book is dedicated to her.

Many of the other authors who came before me are acknowledged by the names of characters in this book. Donovan is named after John Donovan, author of *I'll Get There. It Better Be Worth the Trip,* a YA novel that came out in 1969, the same year as Stonewall, and is widely considered the first openly queer YA novel. Mr. Howe is named after my friend James Howe, whose book *Totally Joe* was the first joyful, unabashedly gay middle-grade novel I ever read. (It's still one of my all-time favorites.) Principal Woodson is named after Jacqueline Woodson, who still inspires me with every book she writes. (My grade school years would have been so much cooler if she'd been my principal.) Ms. Guy is named after Rosa Guy, the author of *Ruby,* considered the first openly queer Black YA novel. Other writers whose names you'll find within the book include Sandra Scoppettone, Michael Cart, Francesca Lia Block, M. E. Kerr, and Jenny Pausacker, all of whom have done mighty work in building the LGBTQIA+ canon for kids and teens. This is by no means an exhaustive list of the authors who were published before my first book, *Boy Meets Boy,* in 2003. But it's a good place to start.

I also want to thank all of my LGBTQIA+ author peers, and all of the authors who debuted after I did—I delight in the fact that there are far too many of them for me to name here. I want to give a special shout-out to Alex Gino, whose middle-grade novels are a joy to me as an editor and an inspiration to me as an author. As I'm writing this in 2021, Alex has been at the top of the American Library Association's annual list of the ten most challenged books for three years in a row. In 2018, their book was joined by seven other LGBTQIA+ titles, including my own *Two Boys Kissing.* This past year, it was joined by *Stamped,* Jason Reynolds's YA version of Ibram X. Kendi's *Stamped from the Beginning,* and a number of other antiracist books, as well as Laurie Halse Anderson's *Speak* and Toni Morrison's *The Bluest Eye,* for their honest portrayals of abuse. This only shows that the fight against censorship continues on many fronts.

When people attack books, they think the books will not be able to defend themselves. Luckily, there are many, many people who step in to defend not just the books but the people in the community whom the books are about. Authors, myself included, are emboldened to write freely because we know there are such fierce defenders of the right to read. Thank you to the National Coalition Against Censorship (ncac.org), the Freedom to Read Foundation (ftrf.org), and the American Library Association and its Office for Intellectual Freedom (ala.org), which are among the many fantastic organizations on the front lines helping students, teachers, librarians, parents, publishers, and authors defend the right to read.

I don't want to give the people who attack LGBTQIA+ literature and identities too much space, because the truth of the matter is that our stories should never be defined by the people who don't want us to tell them. Instead, they should be defined by the millions of readers of all ages who take them to heart. Like a first Pride parade, or the first time you make a friend who identifies the same way you do, the first time you find yourself in a book is a powerful moment—and many of us have taken the power we've experienced as readers and used it to create our own stories. This path can be as wide as we make it, and as long as we want it to be.

Be a part of what comes next.

ACKNOWLEDGMENTS

Thank you to my mother and father. You built my moral compass.

Thank you to my teachers. Fifth grade was truly my magical year, and Dr. O'Desky and Dr. Brenner were the reason. (That's one person. She got married halfway through the year.)

Thank you to my Uncle Jack for reading everything I've written the day it's come out, if not before.

Thank you to Grandma Grace for collecting turtles.

Thank you to the friends who were present in the room (or somewhere else in the house) as this book was being written, especially Mike Ross, who was present when I rediscovered the opening I'd written four years prior and then pretty much forgot was on my computer. (Thanks to my four-years-prior self for getting things started, too. Fellow writers, let this be a lesson to always keep the fragments around.) Thanks to Nick Eliopulos and Zack Clark, whose Adventurers are more fantastical than mine. Thanks to Billy Merrell for being Billy Merrell. Thanks to Andrew Eliopulos, simply because when I thought of who the ideal audience for this book was, the answer was Andrew Eliopulos. And thanks to Regina Spektor, because when I was in search of a title, the first song I thought of was "Us" . . . and there it was.

Thank you to Tiernan Bertrand-Essington, who's heard me talk cryptically about this book for a while. I'm happy you can finally read it.

Thank you to everyone who fights for the freedom to read, including all of the organizations mentioned in the author's note. Thank you to both the publisher of this book, Penguin Random House, and the publisher where I work, Scholastic, for being champions of both books and authors. Special thanks to Dick Robinson from Scholastic for a lifetime of support.

Thank you to Marisa DiNovis, Melanie Nolan, Barbara Marcus, Mary McCue, and the entire Random House family, with a special shout-out to Adrienne Waintraub and her team because this is a book about free expression. Thank you to Bill Clegg and everyone at the Clegg Agency. And last and never, ever least—thank you to Nancy Hinkel, who makes sure the words are all in the right place. I need you like the moon needs poetry.